Bello:

hidden talent rediscovered

Bello is a digital only imprint of Pan Macmillan,
established to breathe new life into previously published,
classic books.

At Bello we believe in the timeless power of the imagination,
of good story, narrative and entertainment and we want to use
digital technology to ensure that many more readers
can enjoy these books into the future.

We publish in ebook and Print on Demand formats
to bring these wonderful books to new audiences.

www.panmacmillan.co.uk/bello

Margaret Pemberton

Margaret Pemberton is the bestselling author of over thirty novels in many different genres, some of which are contemporary in setting and some historical.

She has served as Chairman of the Romantic Novelists' Association and has three times served as a committee member of the Crime Writers' Association. Born in Bradford, she is married to a Londoner, has five children and two dogs and lives in Whitstable, Kent. Apart from writing, her passions are tango, travel, English history and the English countryside.

Margaret Pemberton

THE MYSTERY
OF SALIGO BAY

BELL

First published in 1976 by Macdonald and Jane's

This edition published 2013 by Bello
an imprint of Pan Macmillan, a division of Macmillan Publishers Limited
Pan Macmillan, 20 New Wharf Road, London N1 9RR
Basingstoke and Oxford
Associated companies throughout the world

www.panmacmillan.co.uk/bello

ISBN 978-1-4472-4462-2 EPUB
ISBN 978-1-4472-4461-5 POD

Visit **www.panmacmillan.com** to read more about all our books
and to buy them. You will also find features, author interviews and
news of any author events, and you can sign up for e-newsletters
so that you're always first to hear about our new releases.

To my Mother and Father

Chapter One

The road curved round the head of the loch, narrow and windswept. Torrential rain poured down on to the surrounding moorland of peat and heather, and sheep huddled dejectedly together, seeking what shelter they could. In the distance the flat expanse of the sea, grey and desolate, surged beneath heavy clouds. A lone farmhouse braced itself against the elements, the carefully planted trees that surrounded it bent almost double by the driving wind and rain. Islay offered a forbidding welcome. Garden of the Hesperides Miranda had called it, but Miranda was dead and the storm-wracked day matched Sally's mood perfectly.

This was Sally Craig's first visit to the Hebrides and it was not one she had wanted to make. The drive from London had been long and arduous, and the two-and-a-half-hour sail from the mainland to Port Askaig had been rough and unpleasant. As soon as the ferry had left the shelter of the coast, the storm had broken and the Atlantic crosswind had smacked hard. Sally shuddered. In all her twenty-four years she had never felt quite so ill and dejected. But then, if the journey had been under different circumstances, perhaps even that wouldn't have been so bad . . .

The windscreen wipers flicked backwards and forwards and through the streaming rain could be seen a string of whitewashed cottages and the blurred signpost of Bruichladdich.

A stone-built jetty with a handful of fishing boats anchored in its lee, a village shop and a large building that was the local distillery, came and went and the hamlet was submerged once more in incessant rain. The barren moorland gave way to cultivated fields of wheat, lying sodden and saturated beneath the relentless downpour of rain.

Sally squinted into the distance. Surely Port Charlotte couldn't be much further? If it was, then there wasn't much likelihood of her reaching it. Another ten minutes and the road would be flooded and the car immobile. She frowned. Perhaps this whole journey was a waste of time, nothing but the product of an overworked imagination ... Miranda's last letter lay heavy in her pocket and the frown deepened.

Sally had known Miranda Taylor since she was seven years old, when Miranda and her parents had moved into the adjoining cottage on the outskirts of Little Feltham. Little Feltham had never seen anything quite like the Taylors before. Their household consisted of several large dogs, two ponies, and an assortment of guinea-pigs and rabbits. The small rooms of the period cottage were transformed into a private zoo, not helped by the half-finished pottery, easels, sculpture and other discarded remains of each new hobby that Mrs Taylor picked up and dropped with alarming dexterity. To Sally, an only child of conventional parents, the chaos was fascinating.

Miranda had been a long-legged tomboy, full of confidence and daring and Sally had been lost in admiration. It was Miranda who got them into scrapes, Sally who got them out. They had made a solemn pact to be best friends, and best friends they had remained. By the time the girls reached school-leaving age it was obvious that Little Feltham would not hold Miranda for long, and for the first time in ten years they parted. Sally went respectably to read English Literature at University and Miranda went to Rome, ostensibly to be a companion to her mother's older sister, Countess Rissaro, who had been recently widowed.

From the letters Sally received at Oxford, it was clear that the bereavement had not plunged Miranda's aunt into deep mourning, and with her new-found independence and the conveniently large sum that her husband had so considerately left behind him, the Countess and her niece proceeded to enjoy life. Sally joined them for her holidays the following year and found a very different Miranda from the one she had previously known.

The exuberance and vitality were still there, but under her aunt's careful supervision Miranda had been transformed from an attractive eighteen-year-old with good legs into a raving beauty. She was slimmer than when she had left Little Feltham, and above the perfect cheek-bones the dark eyes looked huge. Her auburn hair was now a glossy black, swinging thickly to her shoulders, and her dress was of scarlet silk, rich-looking and sophisticated. Sally, although a pretty girl herself, felt almost plain in comparison. But despite the change in Miranda's looks there had been none in Miranda herself. The girls were just as close as they had ever been, and there were tears on both sides when Sally had returned in the autumn to Oxford.

Mrs Craig viewed her daughter apprehensively the next time she came home, searching for any signs of unrest or discontent after weeks of Miranda's company under the hot Italian sun. To her relief she found none.

'Sally,' she confided to her husband, 'is such a nice *level-headed* girl, far too sensible to behave like Miranda.'

Her husband had raised an enquiring eyebrow and she had added hastily: 'Not that I think Miranda is *misbehaving* herself in Rome, but the Taylors' standards *are* different from ours, and it's such a relief not to have to worry about Sally doing anything rash or foolhardy.'

Unaware of her mother's remarks, Sally had returned to University and her studies. Mrs Craig would have blanched if she had heard her daughter in the debating society, or had been aware of the number of young men anxious to know Sally a little more intimately, but though she had plenty of boy-friends there was none serious enough to have caused Mrs Craig any worry.

It was Miranda who did that.

The year Sally left University, Miranda left Rome. Her aunt had re-married and her niece and new husband were not compatible. After a brief week in Little Feltham, Miranda packed her bags once more and, much to Mrs Craig's relief, left on the night train to London. It was a relief that was short-lived. To her dismay Sally announced her intention of joining Miranda.

For the first time Mrs Craig realized that her daughter, apart from being a nice girl, was also stubborn. Her pleadings were in vain, Sally was firm. She was twenty-two, had found a good job with a large advertising agency in Knightsbridge, and was not, as her mother insisted, heading for a fate worse than death. Mrs Craig bowed to the inevitable and bought her daughter a travelling clock for a going-away present.

Despite the differences in the girls' temperaments, the arrangement worked well. Miranda did a three-month modelling course and Sally began work at Carter and Leach. Their life resembled that of thousands of other girls sharing flats and bedsitters.

Until Miranda met Jeff Roberts.

He was a photographer who did a lot of work for Sally's firm and it was through her they met. He was twenty-eight, aggressively handsome, with dark hair and high Slav cheek-bones. He didn't give a damn for anyone's opinion but his own, was full of brash confidence in his own ability, which was considerable, and had a bad reputation where women were concerned. His meeting with Miranda was explosive.

Within weeks Miranda had made the coveted cover of a glossy magazine, and from then on did solely photographic work, spending as much time in Paris and New York as she did in London.

If Mrs Craig shook her head with worry at the sight of Miranda lounging elegantly outside an ancestral home with a couple of Borzoi dogs on a gold lead, her friend, who knew her rather better, didn't.

Or rather, they didn't until Miranda went to Turkey.

The whole idea of the trip was to promote Lee Domini's new collection of evening clothes with the ruined city of Ani as background. Jeff was in America and Miranda took advantage of the fact by deciding to prolong her stay. Jeff, she said, would have to cancel their engagements for June, she was going to lounge by the Black Sea for a month. Jeff, when he returned, was furious. He sent telegram after telegram but all he received back were glowing accounts of mountains and forests and Byzantine ruins. Then, to make matters worse, Miranda wrote saying she wouldn't be flying back but was driving home in Tony Carpenter's Range Rover.

'What the hell,' Jeff had shouted, waving the letter before Sally's face, 'is she doing with Tony Carpenter?'

Sally had frowned. 'Nothing as far as I know. I saw him with Gregory Phillips in Tattersall's only last week.'

He thrust the letter into her hand ungraciously.

'What's his bloody Range Rover doing in Turkey in the first place? Miranda must be out of her mind. By the sound of her letter it will be Christmas before we see her again, and meanwhile I'm losing thousands of pounds worth of work, the silly, stupid . . .'

'You've not read it properly. Tony Carpenter *isn't* in Turkey. Miranda says here his brother drove out there last April to join an archaeological dig and wants to stay longer than he first said. He took Tony's car and not unreasonably Tony would like it back again and when Miranda told him she was going there, he asked her if she liked the idea of driving it back. Simple really.'

'Simple? *Simple?* You mean that effeminate slob talks my model into skiving off for weeks on end doing *him* favours . . .'

'She wouldn't have done it if she hadn't wanted to,' Sally said reasonably.

He swung round. 'You're just as bad. Hare-brained, irresponsible . . .'

Sweeping up his jacket he'd whirled out of the flat, slamming the door behind him.

It had been the second week in August when Miranda had returned. London had been in the grip of a sweltering heat wave and Sally had arrived home from work, hot and tired, to find Miranda in the bath and her clothes scattered the length and breadth of the flat. Instead of being wildly enthusiastic about her trip, she had seemed vaguely preoccupied and pensive. It was such a startling contrast to the usual Miranda that Sally wondered if she was having qualms at the high-handed way she had treated Jeff.

He had been round at the flat by eight o'clock, yelling that she was nothing but a country amateur and he'd never photograph her again even if he was starving, and Miranda yelled back that if he didn't photograph her, starve was exactly what he would do. It wasn't an evening Sally cared to remember. Jeff had stormed out of the flat, and Miranda, complaining of a headache, had gone straight to bed.

The next day she was still unusually quiet and before Sally left for work she asked her to ring Jeff and give him a message.

'You mean you're not going to the studio?' Sally asked, surprised. 'He didn't mean a thing he said last night. He'll expect you to be there . . .'

Miranda rested her chin on her hands and said, 'Well, I'm not going. Not today.'

Sally stared at her in perplexity. 'Are you ill?'

Miranda smiled and shook her hair away from her face. 'No, I'm not ill, Sally. But I can't face Jeff. Not today.'

Sally hesitated, then picked up her jacket. 'I haven't time to argue with you now, I'm going to be late. I'll see Jeff, but he's going to hit the roof. I'll tell him you're not feeling well.'

Sally slipped round to the studio in her lunch hour and Jeff was busy dismantling his equipment. When she gave him Miranda's message he didn't say anything, but kept on working, the lines around his mouth grim and firm.

Sally said uncomfortably, 'I'm sure she'll ring you tomorrow. She really isn't well, she's hardly said a word since she came home. She's not acting a bit like her usual self . . .'

'You've no need to apologize for her. I told her we were through last night and I meant it.'

'Oh, rubbish!' Sally said exasperatedly. 'You're behaving as though you've had a lovers' quarrel!'

With studied care he began to pack his cameras into leather covers and she watched him . . . wondering. It had always surprised her that Miranda's and Jeff's relationship had remained platonic for so long. Jeff, despite his brusque manner, had charm, and even Sally, who always felt uncomfortable in his presence, had to admit he was handsome. Not in the classical sense, he was too swarthy for that, with deep lines running from nose to mouth and a wide, mobile mouth that looked as if it should laugh a lot but didn't. Miranda had said he was twenty-eight, but he could have been older. He was tall and slenderly built with something about his movements that suggested he could take care of himself if he needed to. And if Miranda's stories were to be believed, he'd had to do that quite a lot in the years before he came to London. Miranda said he'd been brought up in New York by an aunt after his parents had been killed in a car crash and that there was more to Jeff Roberts than met the eye.

He said suddenly, 'I've got two tickets for the première of *Tornado*. I'll pick you up about seven o'clock.'

For a second she was speechless. In all the time she had known him he had never shown her the slightest attention and his offer coming now in such a peremptory fashion confirmed what she had been thinking: that the relationship between Miranda and himself had changed and that they had quarrelled. There were several girls in the agency he had taken out once or twice and then virtually ignored. She said without thinking, 'The more I see you, Jeff Roberts, the less I like you.'

He was lifting out a light bulb and his hand stopped in mid-air. He said in genuine astonishment, 'What the hell made you say that?'

She flushed, saying coolly, 'I'm sorry, I hadn't realized I was speaking out loud.'

'Oh, thanks a lot,' he said, sitting down on the edge of a table. 'That makes me feel a lot better. Just how long have I been the object of such dislike?'

'Now you're being foolish.'

'No, I'm not,' he said, eyes blazing. 'Damn it. You walk in here your normal, friendly self, then suddenly say you can't stand the sight of me!'

'That wasn't what I said.'

'Maybe not the exact words but the gist of it is the same. Perhaps you'll pay me the courtesy of telling me why?'

'I doubt if you'd understand.' She hardly understood herself why this man should arouse such contradictory feelings in her.

He slid off the table and for a moment she thought he was going to strike her, then he said between his teeth, 'No, I probably wouldn't. But I'll understand in the future.' He pulled her roughly towards him and kissed her hard.

For a brief second she was so shocked that she didn't resist, then she struggled free, letting fly with her right hand, the palm stinging against the side of his face. He let her go and hurriedly she turned and made for the door.

Fuming, she marched down the passageway and out into the King's Road. Jeff Roberts was the most arrogant, conceited and presumptuous man she had ever met. Tears of anger stung the back of her eyes and she blinked them away, scanning the road for an empty cab. By the time she reached the office the violence of her feelings had subsided, but she resolved that she would have a straight talk with Miranda that evening. There had never been any secrets between them before, and if something was worrying Miranda she wanted to know what it was ... especially if that something was Jeff Roberts.

Sally was in the kitchen when Miranda arrived home that evening.

'Is there any hot water?' she called from the door as it slammed shut behind her. Then, without waiting for Sally's reply, she threw her coat over a chair, dropped her hat on to the floor and whirled into the bathroom, saying: 'If the phone rings, I'm not in. Not to anyone. Understand?'

'And will you be?' Sally asked a few minutes later, picking up the hat and walking into the bathroom after her.

'Yes, just for once, I will be.' She smiled at Sally affectionately as the water gushed amidst clouds of steam into the bath. 'You're not going out, are you?'

Sally shook her head.

'Good,' Miranda said, pinning her hair on top of her head and stepping into the pine-scented water. 'We can have an evening at home.'

'And talk?' Sally suggested.

Miranda slid down amongst the foam. 'Darling Sally, we can talk all night if you wish, but if anyone should call I'm not at home.' She closed her eyes. 'If you knew how glorious this bath is . . .' The door bell rang and her eyes flew open in alarm.

Sally waved a hand soothingly. 'Don't worry. I'll send them on their way.'

Humming to herself she walked down the hallway and opened the door. The figure in the dusk was tall and unmistakably that of Jeff Roberts.

'What the . . .' she began, and made to shut the door.

'Don't get excited,' he said coolly. 'I came to see Miranda, not you,' and he put his weight against the door, forcing it open. She ran after him as he strode down the hall.

'Miranda is out . . .' she began.

He said coldly, 'Lie to anyone else, but not to me.' Then he called loudly: '*Miranda!*'

'I've told you she is out, now will . . .'

'Be with you in a minute, Jeff,' Miranda's voice answered. 'Help yourself to a drink.'

Furiously Sally turned her back on him and marched into the bathroom. Struggling to control her temper she said, 'You distinctly told me you weren't in to anyone.'

'Well, I'm not,' said Miranda, surprised. 'But Jeff isn't anyone, is he?'

'Apparently not,' Sally replied witheringly. 'Perhaps you should make your instructions a little clearer in future, let me know if there are any exceptions to your rules.'

'Sally!' Miranda stopped soaping her leg and stared at her in amazement. 'What on earth is the matter?'

'Nothing that a little fresh air won't cure. I'm walking over to Greenwich Park. We'll talk later, when that impossible Jeff Roberts has gone.'

Sally went into her bedroom and put on her coat, then let herself quietly out of the flat. Hands buried deep in her pockets she strode across the heath and towards the park, until her temper had abated. Tonight, without fail, she would ask Miranda if there was anything new in her relationship with Jeff Roberts. And surprised herself by hoping fervently that the answer would be no.

Chapter Two

It was a warm evening and the heath was bespattered with courting couples and children. She paused at the pond to watch two grubby little boys sailing a homemade boat. She was so engrossed in her own thoughts that she did not at first hear her name being called. When it finally penetrated her consciousness she turned her head, and there, leaning out of his car window, was Gregory Phillips. Although he was a close friend of Tony Carpenter's, and moved in the same circles as Miranda, Sally did not know him very well.

As she approached the car he said with a smile, 'I've just been to the flat. But no one was in. You don't know where Miranda is likely to be, do you?'

'No,' Sally said vaguely.

He looked annoyed and sat biting his lip for a second. Then he said, 'I'm going for a meal, care to join me?'

She hesitated for a moment then decided that having dinner with Gregory would be far more pleasant than wandering about by herself, tormented by her thoughts of Miranda and Jeff. She was sure they were still in the flat and simply ignoring the bell.

Gregory Phillips was dark and good-looking and knew it. He was somewhere in the region of thirty, tall and well-built with a sophisticated charm that somehow failed to charm Sally.

'I couldn't get Miranda on the phone today either. She isn't abroad, is she?' Gregory asked as soon as she was seated beside him.

'No. I think she's just feeling a little anti-social. Can I give her a message?'

'No, I'd like to see her myself. Where is she working tomorrow?'

Sally frowned. 'I think she mentioned a show at the Savoy but I'm not sure.'

His gaze flickered from the road, meeting hers. 'Or she may be in when I return to the flat after dinner?'

'Yes,' Sally said, 'she may.'

His eyes held hers for so long that Sally was terrified they would have an accident, then he said: 'You know Tony Carpenter, don't you? He's over at "Felipe's". You don't mind if we join him?'

'No,' Sally said, beginning to wonder if she wouldn't have been wiser to continue her lonely walk. All she knew of Tony was that it was his brother who was in Turkey, and that Miranda had brought his Range Rover back for him. She said hesitantly, 'I'm not really dressed to go out for dinner. Is "Felipe's" that kind of place?'

He gave her a cool appraising stare, then he said: 'Nonsense! You look beautiful.'

Sally turned her eyes to the view of street lights outside, wishing more than ever that she had refused his invitation. She had a vague memory of Miranda once saying that she didn't like Gregory Phillips and her unease deepened.

The restaurant was by the river and decorated in fresh greens and whites, without a romantic candle in sight, much to Sally's relief. Gregory steered her to a corner table where Tony already sat, sipping a drink. His eyebrows rose imperceptibly when he saw her and then he smiled.

'This is a nice surprise,' he said.

'Yes, isn't it? I'm afraid Gregory was wanting to see Miranda really. I'm just a substitute.'

Gregory laughed, saying in explanation, 'I'd gone to the flat to see Miranda but she was out. As I was coming back across the heath I saw Sally and, not being a man to throw away opportunities, persuaded her to join us.'

'I'm glad you did,' Tony said amiably. 'Isn't it the première of *Tornado* tonight? I expect Miranda is attending it. The producer is an old boy-friend, isn't he?'

Sally avoided his eyes and said lightly, 'I've really no idea.'

Gregory said smoothly, 'I'm sure Miranda would have mentioned it to Sally if she had been going. I've a feeling she will be in by the time I take Sally home.'

As they talked Sally studied Tony Carpenter. He was older than herself, probably in his mid-thirties, though he took pains not to make it obvious; he was tall and slim and used his hands in an affected manner when talking, but she felt that though Jeff Roberts had labelled him as effeminate, it wasn't the case. Although his hair was a nondescript mousy brown and thinning, it was perfectly cut, and she guessed the loss caused him some pain. He was fine-boned with a delicate face for a man and a rather prissy mouth. His long, thin fingers were carefully manicured and there was a sweet smell of perfume about him.

'Do try the Soupe à l'Oignon,' he said suddenly. 'It's delicious.'

'And the grouse,' Gregory added. 'They serve it with lettuce stuffed with honey and mint. Very original.'

'Is your brother still in Turkey?' Sally asked, as he passed her the menu.

'Oh yes, digging away for antiquities. Not my scene at all. I expect Miranda has told you all about the excavations?'

'No, we haven't had a chance to talk yet. I've hardly seen her since she came back, she has an enormous amount of work to catch up on.'

'Ah yes, it isn't all *la gloire*, is it?' Tony said cheerfully.

'Apparently Miranda is feeling anti-social at the moment,' Gregory interrupted, and Tony's eyelids flickered in surprise.

'Really? I haven't heard from Scott since she left Turkey, either. It must be catching.'

'Is Scott your brother?' Sally asked.

'Yes.' He grinned at her. 'And quite a lady-killer when he's not grubbing about in tombs and catacombs. I hope Miranda didn't meet her match.'

He and Gregory began talking about Scott, while Sally drank her soup, wondering if Scott Carpenter and not Jeff Roberts was the cause of Miranda's preoccupation.

Tony said, 'Are you and Miranda cousins?'

Sally smiled. 'No, though many people think we are. We grew up together and have always been friends. When we were children we used to pretend we were sisters, and that is how we think of ourselves.'

'Has Miranda any other family?' Gregory asked and Sally said, 'No, only her parents,' wondering why Miranda's relations should be of any interest to him.

There was a short silence and then Sally asked, 'Are you in the rag trade, Tony?'

'Good heavens, no. I dabble in antiques, buying and selling, a bit of this and a bit of that, anything to keep the wolf from the door.'

'Is your shop in town?' Sally asked.

'I don't have one. I handle most things privately. Would you like some more wine?'

Sally declined, wondering what other topic she could bring up. Despite their friendliness, she did not feel at ease. Gregory solved the problem by saying: 'What time do you think Miranda will be back?'

'I really don't know, Gregory. Are you sure I couldn't give her a message, ask her to ring you in the morning?'

'No, I'd rather see her myself.'

'What is it that is so important?' Sally asked, as the waiter set a plate in front of her.

There was the tiniest pause and then he said, 'Business. If Miranda agrees we could do both ourselves a good turn.'

He didn't elaborate, and Sally lapsed into silence, conscious of the fact that Gregory looked repeatedly at his watch. She wondered if it had been Gregory Miranda wished to avoid this evening, and remembering that Miranda disliked him, resolved not to let him into the flat when he took her home.

'I wouldn't build up your hopes, Gregory. Sometimes I don't see Miranda for days on end. I hope it doesn't prove to be a wasted evening for you.'

He put his hand over hers, saying softly, 'My dear Sally, I'm sure it won't be.'

She withdrew her hand, carefully avoiding his eyes, wishing once again that she hadn't accepted his offer and that she didn't have to face the journey home alone with him.

Inevitably the plates disappeared and the small talk diminished. Tony finished his wine and said, 'I'm afraid I'll have to be going, so I'll leave you two on your own now. I'll give you a ring tomorrow, Gregory, and it's been lovely seeing you again, Sally. Do give my love to Miranda. Tell her I'm having a party tomorrow night and that I hope you'll both be there. 'Bye for now.'

'Would you like some more wine?' Gregory asked when Tony had gone, his leg brushing lightly against hers.

'No, thank you.'

'Then perhaps we should be going as well.' Having paid the bill, he stood up and they went to collect Sally's coat. As he slipped it over her shoulders, his hands lingered on the nape of her neck and her heart sank. She hoped fervently that she would be able to escape from the car into the flat without another unwelcome embrace. First Jeff Roberts and now Gregory Phillips. Two unwelcome embraces in one day would be too much.

The warmth of the car and the soft music from the radio gave the atmosphere a false intimacy and Sally did her best to destroy it by chattering about her work. His arm slid round her shoulder as the car halted outside the flat. She reached for the door handle, saying brightly, 'I'll just see if Miranda's in. The hall light is on but that doesn't mean anything. It's always left on.'

His hand tightened its grip and he whispered her name, but she already had the door open, slipped from his grasp and was running up the short flight of steps to the front door. Whether Miranda was in or not, she was determined that Gregory Phillips wasn't setting one foot across the threshold. As her key turned in the lock she heard the car door slam and the sound of hurrying footsteps behind her. In a second she was inside and as he panted to the top step she said with a gay smile, 'Thank you for a lovely meal, Gregory. It really was a pleasant surprise. Miranda isn't in yet, but I'll ask her to phone you.'

'What the hell . . .' he began, as she shut the door firmly in his face.

He banged on the door, but she walked resolutely away and into the kitchen. She heard him swear with disgust and then a minute or two later there came the faint sound of his car engine starting up and she breathed a sigh of relief.

'And just what,' Miranda asked, walking out of the bedroom, 'was all that?'

'*That* was Gregory Phillips. In search of you. Some business deal or other.'

Miranda laughed. 'I take it Gregory was his usual lecherous self. You can ring him tomorrow and tell him I'm out of the country and you don't know where I am.'

Sally looked scornful. 'He's not going to believe that. If he wants to see you, he'll be able to find you easily enough.'

'Oh no, he won't,' Miranda said triumphantly. 'I'm going to Islay for a few days, and while I'm there I want a complete rest. No telephone calls from agents and the Gregory Phillipses of this world. You're the only one who knows where I'll be, and I'm depending on you to keep it quiet.'

Sally could not help it. 'And Jeff Roberts?' she said. 'Does he know where you'll be?'

Miranda shook her hair over her shoulders. 'No, he doesn't, and don't you tell him.'

Sally, envisaging the trouble this would cause, sat down, while Miranda chattered on unconcernedly, busily throwing her clothes into her suitcase and scooping all her toiletries into her overnight bag. Then Sally said slowly, 'Miranda, please tell me if there is anything wrong, anything that is bothering you. You haven't been the same since you got back from Turkey.'

'Don't be a goose,' Miranda said affectionately. 'There's nothing for you to worry about. I've got a personal problem that I have to solve myself. Once I've sorted it out you'll be the first to know. But at the moment I need to be by myself, to think . . . Come on, help me put this little lot into the car.'

Sally stared unbelievingly. 'You mean you're going *now?*'

'Yes, and as the train leaves in forty-five minutes we'd better get a move on. That is, if you're going to see me off—and you will, of course.'

Knowing it was useless to argue with her, Sally helped pile the luggage into the car, and climbed in beside Miranda. As they gathered speed across the heath she looked back and caught sight of the distinctive shape of a Range Rover pulling up beneath the street lights outside the flat. She tapped Miranda's arm.

'Have you time to go back? It looks as if we have company.'

'Not tonight we haven't. Mr Carpenter is out of luck.' And she accelerated, whipping through the narrow streets of Blackheath village with scant regard for other traffic. When they reached the comparative safety of the Old Kent Road, Sally said tentatively, 'Was his brother attractive?'

Miranda changed gear. 'Yes, as a matter of fact he was. But not so much that I fell in love with him, if that is what you're thinking. I do wish you would stop worrying, Sally.'

'But . . .'

'No, Sally, I don't want to talk about it now. It's a decision I have to reach by myself. Two or three days in Islay and the whole thing will seem quite simple. I should be back by the beginning of next week, possibly sooner. We'll have a good old chat then. Just do me a favour and don't tell anyone where I am.'

'Not even Jeff?'

'*Especially* Jeff.'

'And you'll write?'

'Good heavens, Sally, I'm only going away for a few days, but yes, if it will make you feel any better, I'll write.'

Sally stared out of the window glumly. 'Tony Carpenter is having a party tomorrow night. I think I might go along.'

'Now *that's* a good idea. Far better than staying in by yourself.'

Sally stared at her friend's profile for a minute or two, then said: 'Gregory Phillips will be there as well. You don't like him, do you?'

'No,' Miranda said lightly, 'I don't.'

Sally lapsed into silence until they reached Kensington Olympia and the waiting train. Miranda was travelling to Stirling, then driving to Kennacraig in Argyllshire to catch the ferry across to Islay. With a strong sense of disquiet, Sally went on board with her to say goodbye. Miranda dropped a mink jacket carelessly down on the seat and grasped Sally firmly by both arms.

'*Do* cheer up. I'm the one with a problem, not you. And I shan't have that for much longer. It's impossible to stay in Islay and be careworn. It's heaven on earth. We'll go there together in the spring, Sally. You'll love it. It's a place of shifting light, with clouds scudding over purple heather and golden gorse and lush meadows thick with flowers and Saligo Bay with Atlantic breakers creaming over silver sands, and seals, and eagles, and friendly faces, and why I prefer this I'll never know.'

She paused for breath, tapping the glossy magazine in her hand with her face on its cover, then she tossed it away, the thin gold bracelets on her wrist jangling and tinkling. 'It was Rome that spoiled me. I'll never make a country girl now.' And she laughed. 'Five days will be super, but quite long enough. Just do me one favour. Don't tell a soul where I've gone. Promise.'

'I promise.'

The whistle blew and Sally scrambled hastily back on to the platform, waving till the slender figure at the window had disappeared from sight before hailing a taxi to take her home.

She had kept her word. She had told no one where Miranda had gone. But three days later it hadn't mattered any more.

Miranda had been drowned with Gregory Phillips in Saligo Bay.

Chapter Three

Sally was brought sharply back to the present as the car skidded round a bend into a village street. Presumably this was Port Charlotte, and she slowed down, fumbling for the piece of paper with the address of the Taylors' holiday cottage on it—An Cala, Port Charlotte. She tried to peer up at the house names through the blurred and streaming glass but they were impossible to see. On the opposite side of the road she could see the yellow sign of an AA hotel swinging wildly in the wind, and she parked in front of it. An Cala could wait till she'd had a warm drink and was better fortified to search for it.

The bar was crowded, so she went into the lounge where a group of five people, wearing heavy jumpers and stout boots, were peering intently at a large-scale map spread out on the coffee table in front of them. They looked up and smiled when she entered, making disparaging remarks about the rain. She murmured politely back, but was relieved when their attention returned to the map. She had too much on her mind to feel sociable.

The waitress brought her a silver tray with tea and scones, and she leant back in the sofa near the log fire, closing her eyes, succumbing to the heat and her tiredness.

'You *must* see Dunyvaig,' one of the men said loudly. 'There you get the real spirit of the Isles . . .'

'That's because you always take a bottle with you, Charles,' the woman next to him said, laughing. 'He toasts every chief from Angus Mor down . . .'

'Wrong again, Claire. I start from Somerled.'

'I don't care where you start from. We're not going today in this weather.'

'The trouble with you,' her companion said good-naturedly, 'is that you've no staining . . .'

The door of the lounge opened suddenly and Sally felt a cold draught on her legs. She moved them nearer the fire and then became aware that whoever had entered the room was walking slowly towards her. A familiar voice said, 'I suppose I should say it's a surprise, but it isn't.'

Sally's eyes opened, widening in disbelief, and the colour drained from her face, leaving her deathly white. She said weakly, 'Jeff!'

He stopped a foot or so away. There was a pause, then he said: 'Why didn't you tell me you were coming here?'

'I might ask the same of you.'

'You might,' he agreed, helping himself to a scone, 'but that doesn't answer my question. Why have you come?'

'Surely that's my affair,' she said, trying to keep her temper and failing.

He shrugged. 'And you're staying here?'

'No. I'm staying at the cottage.'

He paused then, his eyes holding hers steadily. 'The Taylors' cottage?'

'Of course.' For some unaccountable reason she felt the blood rising in her cheeks.

Since the day he had kissed her, Sally had seen Jeff only once, and that had been at Miranda's funeral. Through the numbness of her own grief, his white, taut face had vaguely penetrated. She had averted her head, and walked away. The last person she wanted to see was Jeff Roberts. Now he was here, rude and as objectionable as usual, and this time there was nowhere to walk away to.

He stared down at her, not looking at all pleased with their unexpected meeting, then he said again, sharply: 'Why didn't you tell me you were coming?'

'I fail to see what business it is of yours!'

Ignoring her anger he sat down, then said, 'I presume you've come to collect her things from the cottage?'

Sally took a deep breath before she said carefully, 'Mrs Taylor is going to sell the cottage. Understandably she doesn't want to have to visit it again herself. I expect there will be some things to take back, but I hadn't really thought about it.'

'Then what *are* you thinking about?' he asked, his voice rising.

The people at the far side of the room turned, listening with interest.

'Don't *dare* talk to me like that, Jeff Roberts. You're the rudest, most ill-mannered man I've ever had the misfortune to meet. It's bad enough being here as it is, without having you making things worse, and . . .' Her voice began to quiver and she stirred her tea vigorously. There was silence for a few moments and when she looked up again, he was smiling, the charm turned full on.

'I apologize. Now, if I ask you nicely, will you please tell me the real reason you're here?'

The anger died within her. 'If I do, will you tell me why *you're* here?'

'Yes. Scouts honour.'

'I came because I don't think Miranda's death was an accident,' she said simply.

'You don't think . . .' He stared at her for a few minutes and then he laughed. 'I take it you're joking?'

'No, I'm not joking, I mean it.'

'My dear Sally, you must be barmy. Of course it was an accident. The coroner said it was an accident. Why should you think any different?'

'Because,' Sally said quietly, 'Miranda wrote me a letter the day before she died.'

Jeff's eyes darkened. 'You're not trying to tell me that Miranda committed suicide.'

'Now *you're* being ridiculous. Miranda was the last person in the world to do that.'

'Then what . . .?'

'I don't *know*.'

'I would suggest, Sally, that you stay here the night and let me take you home tomorrow. The strain has been too much for you . . .'

'No. I've made arrangements to stay at the cottage and I'm going to stay there. I know that I'm right.'

He shook his head and she said angrily, 'You haven't seen the letter. I have. Miranda knew she might die.'

'Then why,' he asked coldly, 'didn't you mention it before?'

She stared back at him miserably. 'She asked me not to tell anyone that she'd written, and at the time I was so shocked at what had happened that I couldn't think clearly. There was nothing *definite* in the letter and . . .'

'Perhaps it would help if you told me what *was* in it.'

Sally leant her head against the back of the chair and twisted the ring on her little finger, her lips firmly closed.

'Oh, come on,' Jeff said, a note of exasperation in his voice. 'This is hardly the time to be coy, is it? Don't forget that Miranda and I worked together for a long time. We were very good friends.'

Sally paused, wanting to ask him if that was all they had been, good friends, but instead she said, 'Miranda said she'd reached the right decision, but that she'd reached it too late.'

'Decision? What decision?'

'That's just it. I don't know. Ever since she came back from the wretched trip to Turkey she'd been tense and nervous, but she wouldn't tell me what it was that was bothering her. That's why she came here, to sort out her problems by herself. She promised me that when she returned she'd tell me everything, but . . .'

'The letter?' he prompted.

She forced herself to meet his gaze. 'Miranda said she'd reached the right decision too late. She was returning to London straight away, and was catching the early morning ferry from Islay to the mainland, but if anything happened to her in the meantime, Pete Mackay would explain. She said she couldn't be any clearer or it would make things difficult for me, and that I wasn't to worry, she felt marvellous, and though she'd over-stepped the mark, she was sure she could handle everything, but on no account was I to tell anyone she had written.'

Jeff's eyes were narrowed, but very keen. 'And who is Pete Mackay?'

'I haven't the faintest idea. That's one of the things I hope to find out.'

'That should be easy enough.'

His tone was light, and Sally could detect no signs of jealousy, but then, even if there had been, Jeff Roberts would not have allowed it to show. She said: 'As far as I'm concerned, that letter indicates that she knew there was a possibility of *something* happening to her . . .'

'It was an *accident*, Sally. The coroner said there had been fatalities at Saligo Bay before. The currents there are strong and there are warning notices to that effect. Swimming there is just the sort of headstrong thing Miranda would do.'

'And Gregory Phillips as well?'

He shrugged. 'Apparently so.'

She shook her head. 'I grew up with Miranda and I knew her better than anyone else. Miranda was headstrong but she wasn't a fool, and what's more, she was an extremely strong swimmer. Her family have been coming to Islay for years now and Miranda knew all the bays, she wouldn't swim in waters she couldn't cope with.'

'But she *did*,' Jeff pointed out reasonably.

Sally's mouth closed in a firm line. 'I don't think so.'

'Then for goodness sake, what *do* you think?'

'That's just it. I don't know.' She paused. 'I'm sure your reason for being here is far more sensible.'

A barely discernible tinge of colour heightened his cheeks but he said calmly, 'Miranda said Islay was worth visiting and so I came.'

'But why now? Just two weeks after her death!' Sally exclaimed scornfully. 'Come off it. What's the real reason?'

There was a pause, then he said: 'Would it sound feasible if I said I was here for the same reasons you are?'

She stared at him, her eyes widening. 'You mean Miranda wrote to you . . .'

He shook his head. 'No, but I felt like you. Why Gregory Phillips?'

She stared at him, wondering once more about his relationship with Miranda. It was on the tip of her tongue to ask him when he said, 'I think the best thing is for you to return to London and let me have a word with Pete Mackay myself.'

Sally rose to her feet. 'It's very considerate of you, but I'd rather not. It's stopped raining now, so I think I'll have a look for the cottage.'

'It's one of the small fishermen's cottages on the shore-line, just beyond the jetty.'

She stared at him, then said suspiciously, 'Just how long have you been in Port Charlotte?'

'Since yesterday.'

'And you've been to the cottage?'

He nodded. 'But I didn't gain access. Mrs MacBride of Harbour Row looks after the place and wouldn't let me so much as peep through the window. I hope you have better luck.'

'Mrs MacBride,' Sally said, 'sounds a sensible woman. Now, which way is it?'

'First left as you leave the hotel, then right. You can't miss it. Be back for seven.'

She bridled at the note of command in his voice. 'Why?'

'Because that's the time dinner is served and I want to talk to you. Don't be late.'

Fuming at his high-handed attitude, but feeling in the circumstances it was easier to agree than to argue, she let him usher her out into the street.

The road to the sea was steep and short and at the foot she could see the stone jetty and seagulls scratching on the narrow belt of shingle, and beyond, the heaving grey-green waves. Gaily coloured fishing boats were pulled up high above the shore-line and children were playing boisterously in and around them, their shouts filling the otherwise empty street. The wind was wet and salt-laden and Sally shivered, digging her hands deeper into her pockets as she turned into the row of neatly kept cottages that faced the sea. Their walls were painted in soft pastel shades and their windows prettily curtained and framed by pots and troughs of flowers. She recognized An Cala as soon as she saw it and faltered.

Miranda had described it to her many times and had planned that they should visit it together, and now she was here, alone. She struggled with herself for a few minutes, the wind tossing her hair and stinging her cheeks. This was the moment of truth. Either she went in and tried to solve the mystery of the last few weeks in Miranda's life, or she headed back to the hotel and dinner with Jeff Roberts and the first ferry home. The latter would be the easier alternative, but then her fingers closed around Miranda's letter and she knew beyond a shadow of doubt that Miranda had wanted her to come, had known that she could rely on her. The feeling of unease crystallized and became a certainty.

Resolutely she grasped the knob of the door and pushed it open.

Chapter Four

Heavy warmth and the faint smell of pine assailed her as she stepped into the shelter of the hallway. She hesitated, aware almost at once of someone else's presence. To the left of her the door opened on to a pleasant room of books and chintz-covered chairs. A grandfather clock in a polished walnut case ticked loudly, the watery sun that now shone weakly through the windows glinting on its glass face. From outside, the insidious sound of the sea beat faintly on the air, rhythmic and insistent.

Soft footsteps hurried through the room behind her and she stiffened, turning quickly, feeling herself an intruder. The plump, aproned figure that opened the far door was infinitely reassuring. A gentle face, pale and lined, smiled welcomingly as she pushed a strand of white hair from her forehead.

'You must be Miss Craig?'

'Yes.'

'I'm Flora MacBride. I've been lookin' out for you. It hasn't been very good weather for your journey, has it?' Without waiting for a reply she said: 'The kettle is on, so you can have a warm drink in a minute. I don't suppose you have used an oil cooker before, have you? Come through an' I'll show you. It's very simple an' it keeps the place lovely an' warm.'

The soft lilting voice paused briefly for breath as she led the way and then she was explaining the mechanics of the cooker, her eyes carefully avoiding Sally's.

The room was long and high and spotlessly clean; a gigantic table lined one side with an old-fashioned creel above it and on the other was the cooker and a dresser full of china and glassware.

Through a half-open door Sally caught a glimpse of a neat, streamlined kitchen and then Mrs MacBride was saying: 'Never turn it below one. You will find it quite easy to use once you get used to it. The immersion heater is in the cupboard in the big bedroom and if you need me for anything I live two doors down.' Their eyes met and the smile flickered, wavered and vanished. She said brokenly, 'I've cleaned the place of course, but everything's in her room exactly as it was . . .'

She sat down heavily, leaning on the table. 'I did everythin' I could . . .' She fumbled for her handkerchief and blew her nose noisily. 'They've been coming here for years, ever since she was twelve. She was like a daughter to me . . . an' now this . . .'

She began to cry and Sally said awkwardly, 'Mrs Taylor wants to close the cottage, as they won't be coming here any more. I thought it would be easier if I came instead of her. She is still terribly shocked.' She hesitated, then said: 'I hoped that by coming I might understand it a little better.'

Mrs MacBride blew her nose again. 'We'd all like to do that, lassie. There's no one understands it, no one at all. Except,' she said with sudden asperity, 'them that have never been here. *They* seem to find it no problem.'

'Did Miranda know anyone, by the name of Pete Mackay?' Sally asked. Mrs MacBride stopped crying and stared at her, her expression one of startled surprise.

'No. Was there any reason why she should?'

Sally hesitated fractionally then said, 'Not really. It was just a name I thought I'd heard her mention. Does a Pete Mackay live in Port Charlotte?'

Mrs MacBride shook her head. 'There's no one of that name here. There's a Patrick Mackay over at Bruichladdich but I don't recall any Peter. Perhaps it was a London friend?'

'I don't think so. I'm quite sure it was someone who lived on the island.'

Mrs MacBride shook her head again. 'There's a lot of Mackays, and no doubt there is bound to be a few Peters among them, but there's none that I know of. Miranda didn't mix with the local boys. More's the pity.'

'Did you meet Mr Phillips often?'

A spasm passed over Mrs MacBride's face and she rose unsteadily to her feet, stuffing her hanky back into her apron pocket. '*Him!*' she said savagely. 'I'd rather not talk about *him*. Nor the others either.' Tears were threatening again. 'That poor, innocent bairn . . .'

'Mrs MacBride . . .' Sally began, but Mrs MacBride was no longer listening; she was staring into the middle distance. She gave herself a shake and said abruptly, 'There's two pints of milk in the fridge an' if you want me for anythin' else, give me a knock. It's the house with the green door. I'm nearly always in.' She gave a watery smile. 'I hope you'll be comfortable, Miss Craig.'

The door banged after her and the house settled back into silence. Sally brushed her fingertips lightly across the gleaming surface of the table, listening and waiting, but for what?

What could there be in this neat, shining and scrubbed cottage that would give her any inkling as to what was on Miranda's mind when she came here? And who had Mrs MacBride meant by the "others"?

Slowly she walked the length of the room and into the hallway, pausing at the foot of the stairs. Mrs MacBride had said she'd put all Miranda's things in her room. If there was anything to be found, it would be there. From outside came the subdued shriek of seagulls and the dull roar of the sea, but they only emphasized the stillness and growing feeling of isolation that seemed to grow stronger and more palpable with every second.

The shallow stairs curved steeply, and Sally climbed, half-apprehensive of what she might find. The large window that faced her at the head of the stairs gave a wide view of the sea, and for the first time Sally saw that it wasn't the open sea but a big bay. At the far side was the dark, blue-black outline of the rest of the island which the heavy clouds had previously hidden. A pale golden sun now rimmed the silhouetted hills, bathing them in an ethereal light, while the mourning clouds rolled slowly eastwards towards the open Atlantic, the wind ruffling the surface of the water. A big white bird dived suddenly, then wheeled and soared, the light shimmering on wet wings.

Sally turned towards one of the closed doors that faced each other on the tiny landing. This room was not Miranda's. Bunk beds and a single divan lined one wall, and the drawers in the dark wooden chest of drawers were all empty. On the wall were framed photographs of Miranda's parents, taken long before Sally knew them, with Mrs Taylor at the rails of a ship and looking very much like her daughter. Sally closed the door behind her and stood for a few seconds watching the bird as it skimmed the sea again, before entering the other room.

It was small and square with a large double bed beneath the window and books and photographs littering an old-fashioned dressing-table. She sat down on the edge of the bed and pulled open the bottom drawer. It was full of familiar clothes, and Sally steeled herself as she reached out slowly to lay them item by item on the bed beside her.

An hour later the whole contents of the room were in neat piles and she had found nothing of interest. Sweaters and skirts, some jewellery, an expensive gold chain belt that Sally remembered Miranda buying after Jeff's first photograph, a whole drawerful of exquisite French lingerie, two bottles of perfume and a pair of good, plain hogskin gloves, heavily soiled. Sally stared at them nonplussed. Gloves were not an item Miranda usually wore and this pair had seen heavy wear.

She lifted them up lightly and crumbs of dried soil scattered to the floor. Gardening? It didn't fit in with what Sally knew of Miranda and, besides, An Cala didn't have a garden. She laid them down thoughtfully: perhaps Mrs Taylor had left them here, or a summer visitor. The cottage was, after all, let to strangers for most of the year, but it was odd that Miranda hadn't turfed them out of the drawer before putting her own things in, especially in view of their dirty condition.

The top drawer had yielded a little more, but nothing that was of any help. Her toilet bag was there and a few items of jewellery, a packet of tissues and three unused postcards of the island, a writing pad, pen and envelopes and a glossy copy of Norman Mailer's *Marilyn*. Sally stared at them, deflated. There were no letters, nothing to give her a clue as to what had been troubling Miranda. Her handbag had been flown home with her body and there had been nothing of importance in that either. Apart from the usual cosmetics, keys and purse, all there had been was a BOAC leaflet giving times of flights to New York, but as Miranda spent half her working life in America, there was nothing very unusual about that.

Heavy-hearted, Sally laid her friend's things back into the drawers. The only clue left was Pete Mackay. He, at any rate, should be able to clarify matters. If he could be found.

She shivered, suddenly aware of how cold it had become, and glanced at her watch. It was 6.50. She was supposed to be meeting Jeff Roberts at seven o'clock, and she hadn't even washed her face or combed her hair, and all her things were still in the boot of the car which was still parked outside the hotel.

'Damn him!' she muttered angrily, grabbing her handbag and running for the stairs.

He made no reference to her windswept appearance, his only interest was in the cottage and what she might have found there and her conviction grew that his motive for being in Islay was to find out why Gregory Phillips had been with Miranda.

She unfolded her napkin while he said exasperatedly: 'But there must have been *something*.'

'Nothing. Only her clothes and toilet things and a couple of blank postcards.'

'I think I'd better go back with you and look for myself.'

'And what right,' Sally asked quietly, 'have you to go searching through her things?'

He said in a tone that was dangerously soft, 'Every right.'

They stared at each other, then Sally said tensely: 'Just what do you mean by that?'

'I'm the one asking the questions, not you.'

She flung her napkin down on the table and began to rise to her feet, but he grasped her wrist, holding her fast.

'Before you go off in a huff, Sally Craig, just listen to me for a few minutes. You're here because you're not happy about the way Miranda died. I'm here for the same reason. You say you were her best friend for fourteen years and that you knew her better than anyone. Well, I knew her too, and I've as much right to find out what happened on this God-damned island as you have, but the only way either of us is going to find out anything is by working together.'

There was a long silence, then Sally said: 'You're right. I'm sorry.'

He grinned, his whole face changing. 'That's more like it. Now don't you think we could be friends for a while and eat?'

For the first time she became embarrassingly aware of the waitress waiting patiently at a discreet distance. She was the same young girl who had served her with tea and scones and she smiled shyly as she handed them the menu, gazing at Jeff adoringly. It looked as if they would at least be able to count on the support of the female population of Port Charlotte.

'Will ye be havin' the two creams with the sweet?' she asked liltingly after they ordered.

Blankly they stared at each other. 'Two?' Sally asked.

'Aye, fresh cream and ice-cream.'

'Fresh cream, please,' Sally said, and then to Jeff: 'I hope the simple things in life aren't always so complicated!'

'They're not. But I'd better warn you about the cheese.'

She raised her eyebrows and he said, as he poured out a glass of wine. 'The local cheese is reputed to have qualities not usually found in dairy produce.'

'Such as?' she asked suspiciously.

He leant towards her and whispered: 'Aphrodisiac.'

Sally said sarcastically, 'Do you know this by repute or experience?'

The lightheartedness went from his voice as he said, 'By repute only. Can't we drop this cold, aloof attitude? So, all right. I upset you that day at the studio. Well, I'm sorry. But we're neither of us going to accomplish anything if we don't forget about it and start afresh. I can be quite likeable when I want to be.'

Sally, looking across at the devastating eyes, thought that that was probably his trouble, and said coolly: 'All right, but why didn't you tell me you were coming here?'

'Why on earth should I? I knew what a shock Miranda's death had been to you. It wouldn't have helped matters if I'd come round burdening you with suspicions, would it? Especially as they were so tenuous.'

'And now?'

'Now they're not. Miranda's letter lends credence to them. We can ask around for this Pete Mackay in the morning. In a place this size he should be easy to find.'

'Oh goodness, I forgot. I asked Mrs MacBride if she knew him and she said she'd never heard of him! Apparently there's a Patrick Mackay at Bruichladdich, but that's all.'

He frowned. 'Curioser and curioser. You're quite sure it said Pete and not Patrick? Miranda's handwriting was rotten.'

'Positive.' She groped in her handbag for the letter. 'See, it says Pete Mackay quite clearly.'

Jeff took the letter from her hand and read it through thoughtfully. When he handed it back there was a deep frown between his brows.

'Well, there are more people to ask than Mrs MacBride. It looks as though we should make an early start in the morning. It may be a little more difficult than we first thought.'

The fish was followed by venison in a wine sauce and Sally said between mouthfuls. 'That wasn't the only thing she said. I asked her if she'd met Gregory Phillips often and her reaction was very positive.'

'Had she?'

Sally looked sheepish. 'To tell you the truth, I still don't know, but she did say: "*Him!* I don't want to talk about *him*, nor the others either." After that she clammed up and left.'

Jeff stared at her, the knife and fork motionless in his hands.

'Others? What others?'

'That's just it. I don't know. I suppose she meant boyfriends, but

Miranda never came here while we were living in London, and Mrs MacBride said herself that Miranda didn't mix with the local boys. The next time I see her I'll ask her what she meant *and* about Gregory Phillips as well.'

'The proverbial nigger in the woodpile,' Jeff said disparagingly. 'The newspapers said they were lovers, but I don't believe it, not for a minute.' He was speaking more to himself than to Sally, and seeing the expression in his eyes, she said quietly: 'Neither do I, but that is what was said at the inquest and that's how it looked. You can't blame them for jumping to conclusions. And what *was* he doing here?'

'That, Sally, is one of the things I intend to find out. What are you going to do with your car? Leave it parked outside?'

'I don't think that will please the hotel. There's room to park outside the cottage. In fact I ought to move it now. It's been a long day and I haven't even unpacked yet.'

'And I'll pick you up at eight tomorrow.'

'Eight!' exclaimed Sally in horror. 'Nine will be quite early enough.'

'Okay, nine. But be ready.'

There he goes again, she thought, bullying . . .

Small lights twinkled beyond the sea on the black horizon and the rising moon bathed the narrow beach in silver light, the waves creamed in pale foam upon the shingle as she drew up outside the cottage and lifted her case from the boot of the car. In the distance she could hear the suck and slap of water against the jetty and the creaking of boats as they lay at anchor and she paused for a few moments, enjoying the stillness and strangeness of the night, before unlocking the door, and heaving her cases inside.

Her hand searched for the light switch and remained there, frozen, as light flooded the downstairs rooms. Then her legs buckled and she sank slowly down the door till she was hunched on the floor, her fists pressed tightly against her mouth, her eyes riveted on the destruction in front of her.

Chapter Five

Books had been swept from their shelves, drawers and their contents spilled chaotically, chairs overturned, pictures shattered, cushions ripped, curtains rent, upholstery slashed. The carpet had been torn from the floor, glass and china lay in smithereens, even the plants had been pulled from their pots.

Weakly Sally staggered to her feet and walked unsteadily into the kitchen. There, cupboards had been wrenched open, cutlery and crockery lay in scattered fragments. Packets of flour and sugar had been torn, their contents spilled, jars had been emptied, cereals and vegetables thrown on to the formica work top. Everything had been emptied, spilt, shattered.

Numbly she moved among the debris, groping her way towards the stairs. The small bedroom had been bare of contents and the intruders had had to be satisfied with dragging the furniture away from the walls and ripping up the carpet, but Miranda's room was in a state of devastation. The eiderdown and pillows had been slit open and loose stuffing choked the air. The mattress had been hacked at and gashed, the dressing-table splintered by the fury with which the drawers had been dragged out, even the insulating around the immersion heater had been stripped off. Miranda's clothes had been thrown on to the landing, her toiletries, gold belt and stationery swept into a careless heap.

Stupefied, Sally sank on to the mutilated bed and reached slowly for the belt, struggling to sort out her chaotic thoughts. She must go for Mrs MacBride, go for Jeff, but her legs wouldn't support her and she remained where she was, the gold belt slipping through her fingers like a rosary.

How long she remained there she never knew, but when she finally rose to her feet her mind was clear. The motive for the break-in had not been theft, the gold within her hands was proof of that. Someone had been searching for something, and by the destruction around her he'd been desperate. But who, and for what?

Bewildered, she made her way back down the stairs and into the living-room, automatically righting a chair and picking up an armful of books that barred her way. What could anyone possibly have been looking for that necessitated such violence? Or was the slashed upholstery and ripped bedding just that? The wrecking of someone's fury and not a search at all? But fury for what? She began to put the books back, grateful for the fact that at least she had been through Miranda's things and knew that nothing had been taken. She slid a volume of Kafka's *The Trial* on to a shelf and leant back on her heels. Something nagged in the depths of her mind, hovering just out of reach. Mentally she went over the list of things that had been in Miranda's drawer: postcards, stationery, gloves, a new book . . .

That was it! The book! She leapt to her feet with a cry and raced up the stairs into the bedroom, frantically rifling through piles of clothes and peering under the bed, but the book that had been in Miranda's drawer had gone. Breathlessly she leant against the wall. Why in heaven's name had Norman Mailer's *Marilyn* been taken? And if that was what the thief had wanted, why the havoc in the kitchen and the vandalism? Surely if all he'd wanted was a book to read, there'd been plenty on the shelves? Head spinning, she hurried once more down the stairs: the first thing she had to do was to go and tell Mrs MacBride: trying to reason it out by herself was impossible. The more she thought about it, the more ridiculous it seemed.

'The whole thing,' she said to the grandfather clock, 'is the work of a lunatic.' The word lingered uncomfortably, and, remembering she had to sleep in the cottage by herself that night, she shivered, wishing she'd never spoken. She was letting her imagination run away with her. Most burglars caused excessive destruction; they were probably piqued at not finding anything of value to steal and had wrecked the cottage for the sheer joy of it. Stupid of them to have overlooked the belt though . . .

By the time she reached Mrs MacBride's green front door, she had decided the intruders were thieves, rejected it; decided they were vandals, rejected that; and, was back on the theory that they were lunatics who just happened to be Marilyn Monroe fans, when Mrs MacBride opened the door, stopping any further speculation.

'Is something wrong, Miss Craig?'

Sally found to her dismay that her voice was trembling and tearful.

'It's the cottage! It's been broken into, ransacked . . . I went for dinner at the hotel and when I returned the door was open and every room has been turned upside down, but nothing's been taken. At least, nothing that I can see except a book of Miranda's. But the furniture is ruined: they've ripped the chairs and bedding and the crockery is smashed. Oh, it's just dreadful . . .'

Throughout this outburst Mrs MacBride stared, eyes wide with horror, one hand clutching nervously at her throat, and Sally began to wonder if she was going to be any help, and if she wouldn't have done better to have gone for Jeff. For as horrified as Mrs MacBride was, she was showing a distinct lack of surprise at what had happened.

'I knew they'd come back. I knew it!' she said, confirming Sally's suspicions. Her hand jerked convulsively on her throat. 'You must go home, Miss Craig. It isn't safe for you here.'

Firmly Sally stepped inside. 'Perhaps you should tell me what's been happening. It was hardly fair of you to let me stay by myself in the cottage if you had reason to think it would be broken into!'

'But I didn't think that would happen again!' She sat down limply on the arm of a chair. 'Miranda came here by herself on the twenty-third of August. I didn't see too much of her. She wasn't a lassie for stayin' in, but the day after she arrived I met her by the jetty—she'd been over at Kilchoman. George Cameron had given me a couple of fish freshly caught and I gave Miranda one. She asked me if I'd cook it for her and I said, aye, of course, but could I borrow the flat pan from the cottage?

'Well, when we went in there … it was a terrific mess. Books thrown all over the place an' drawers emptied, but she wouldn't let me go for the police. "Don't worry," she said to me, "there's no damage done, no need to bother anyone about it." Well, what could I do? It wasn't my cottage and she never would listen if you tried to give her advice … so I helped her clear it up and tried not to worry too much about in. In fact I thought, like her, that it was probably one of the tourists who come here, found out that the cottage belonged to Miranda Taylor an' had come to do a bit of sight-seeing. I suppose the temptation of it bein' open and no one in was too much for him an' he wanted a souvenir. People can be very funny. Miranda said that sort of thing had happened to her before …

'After that I kept an eye open, but the only person who came here was that Gregory Phillips, Miranda was out but he insisted on waitin' for her, said he was a friend from London and that Miranda was expectin' him. Then, next day, there was the accident …' Her hands moved expressively. 'After that I didn't think about the other thing, until *he* came nosying around. He …'

'Just a minute,' Sally interrupted. 'Who do you mean by "he"?'

'The man from London, askin' a lot of questions, tryin' to get into the cottage.'

'Is that who you meant when I asked you about Gregory Phillips and you said you'd rather not talk about him, or the others either?'

'One of them. There was another boyfriend of Miranda's here as well that she didn't know I knew about. I saw them walkin' towards the old burial ground at Octoford when my sister was takin' me down to her place at Port Allen. They were quite a distance away over the fields, but I knew it was Miranda …'

'And the man?' asked Sally. 'Who was he?'

'He wasn't a local, I could tell by his clothes. And it wasn't Mr Phillips. That was the lassie's trouble—too many different boy-friends. I told my sister long ago that no good would come of it …'

'And it wasn't the man who came asking to see the cottage?'

She shook her head emphatically. 'I'd know *him* anywhere. It wasn't him. What her poor mother must be sufferin' now . . .' She paused, and then said: 'I'd better go with you to have a look at the damage an' this time I'm goin' to report it. It isn't safe for folks to go to sleep at night . . .'

Outside the night breeze was cool and refreshing and Sally turned her face gratefully towards it. She said sympathetically, 'These last two weeks must have been very difficult for you. It was bad enough for us in London, not knowing what had actually happened and waiting for news, but to have been here . . .'

A rough hand touched hers in sympathy. 'Aye, it was bad and it will be for some time yet. The newspaper men didn't help either. They didn't give me a minute's peace those few days after, takin' photographs and askin' questions. No respect they showed, none at all.'

'And Miranda didn't leave any sort of message for me?'

'No, lassie. Why, I'd have told you if she had. I know how close you were. Mrs Taylor said you were like sisters.'

'Yes, we were. She sent me a letter the day before she died, the day you saw her walking to the burial ground, and in it she said that if anything happened to her, Pete Mackay would explain. Perhaps the man with her was Pete Mackay?'

Mrs MacBride stared with uncomprehending eyes. 'As to that, Miss Craig, I don't know. But he wasn't a local boy an' I've never heard the name before.'

'And he didn't come forward at the inquest either . . .'

'No, nor he did, though perhaps it would have looked bad if he had done. I mean, her havin' two boy-friends from London at the same time . . .'

'I don't believe Miranda had one boyfriend here from London, Mrs MacBride, not one.'

'Oh, but she did. I saw them together with my own eyes.'

'But you can't be sure it was a boyfriend: it could have been anyone.'

'And Mr Phillips? *He* was her boy-friend, wasn't he?'

'Was he, Mrs MacBride? Did you ever see them together, holding hands or with their arms around each other?'

'I only saw him that once, while he waited for her, but everyone said he was her boy-friend, though that wasn't the word they used. Her lover it said in the papers.' She began to cry softly. 'Horrible they made her sound, an' she was such a beautiful girl, always had a smile an' a cheery word for you, never treated you like a servant which is what some of them do.'

'Mr Phillips, for instance?'

She nodded. 'Very high-handed attitude he had. The papers said they'd known each other for a year though, so I suppose they must have been right.'

'Rubbish. I'd known him for a year and he certainly wasn't *my* lover.'

Mrs MacBride gave a tremulous smile. 'I'm sure you're right, Miss Craig. But who were the other men, and who keeps breaking into An Cala?'

'I don't know, Mrs MacBride, but if I'm going to find out I need to stay here, so we'd better make it habitable again. While you're having a look at the damage, I'll slip up to the hotel. A friend of mine is staying there and he might be able to give us a hand.'

She left Mrs MacBride at the door and ran up the dark street. It never occurred to her that Jeff wouldn't be there and her heart sank as the receptionist said firmly: 'Mr Roberts went out immediately after dinner. Perhaps you could leave a message?'

'No . . . it doesn't matter.'

But it did. It mattered a lot. Dejectedly she set off back to An Cala and Mrs MacBride, feeling bereft and lonely. Rejected too, although that was absurd. Jeff Roberts was nothing to her . . . he had come here because of Miranda. As she herself had.

Chapter Six

By next morning it was as if she had dreamt it. Birds were singing in an azure sky as she and Jeff walked past the white cottages that sprawled out of Port Charlotte. To the left of them, high crags shelved into the sea, spray soaring like jewelled mist into the air as the waves pounded the rocks. Sally let her hand trail loosely amongst the lush green bracken and thickly massed flowers that waved gently in the breeze at the roadside; rougher grass stretched shorewards, the short, springy turf of the machair and the spiky, coarse sea grass. Low stone walls, nearly hidden by bracken and grass, edged the road as it wound southwards between rising fields and the perpetual breaking of waves upon the cliffs. On the far side of the gulf, the unsullied sands of Laggan Bay curved clearly, silver and gold beneath the shelter of hazy hills. The road began to climb, leaving the fields behind for wild moorland that rolled inland in undulating purples and browns, the heather giving way on the higher ground to bare outcrops of gaunt stone.

Intermittently a Land Rover swept by, forcing them into the grassy banks, and occasionally they passed an isolated smallholding with a meagre field wrested from the bracken and a couple of cows grazing contentedly beside whitewashed walls.

The pure clear air, the sunshine and the healthy exercise of walking did much to restore Sally's good humour, and when Jeff said: 'Now tell me everything again, every little detail without missing out a single thing,' she picked a deep pink campion, twirling it between her fingers, studying it carefully as she said: 'I went straight from the hotel to the cottage . . .'

'And you didn't see anybody else in the street, or hear anyone?'

'Not a soul. I opened the door, put on the light and . . .'

'*That's it!*' Jeff said triumphantly, snapping his fingers together. 'And the door wasn't forced, so it was someone who had or has had access to a key! *That* must narrow the field down a bit. The police must be idiots to miss a thing like that . . .'

'Not exactly,' Sally said sheepishly. 'You see . . .'

'My dear Sal, if a door hasn't been forced, and the windows haven't either, and the place has been entered . . .'

'I didn't lock it.'

'. . . it means that . . . What did you say?'

'I didn't lock it. After all, I was only away for a short time, and it just didn't occur to me that in a place like Islay anyone would break in.'

'Dear heaven,' Jeff said devoutly. 'I don't suppose it did, but it may have occurred to you to *tell* me! I mean, if you forget things like that, what other things are you forgetting?'

'If you will let me continue,' Sally said archly, 'we'll find out. Now, where was I? Oh yes, I put on the light and the whole place had been ransacked.'

'I want to know everything about the state of the rooms.'

'I've told you once, Jeff. I really don't see that it's so important.'

'But it *is*. It will give me some idea of what they were looking for.'

'Then you've already made up your mind that they *were* looking for something and were not just thieves?'

'If you mean, do I think An Cala was broken into and devastated by a thief looking for some good bedtime reading, no, I don't. A child of five could see that someone was looking for something.'

'The policeman wasn't so convinced. He said . . .'

'Let's just concentrate on what you and I know and the state of the cottage. Now . . .'

As meticulously as she could, Sally listed the damage done, going through every room until she came to Miranda's bedroom and the disappearance of the book.

'There seems to be a lot of books in the cottage, Sally. Is it possible that this one was already there when Miranda arrived?'

'I shouldn't think so. The other books are all pretty old, mainly classics and poetry. This one was a new one, the cover on it was fresh, almost new.'

He was silent for a while, dark brows knit together in perplexity, then he said slowly, 'You don't think they *could* have been looking for the book, do you?'

'In flour and sugar bags!' Sally said disparagingly.

He gestured impatiently. 'Not the book itself. Something that was *in* the book.'

'Photographs of Marilyn Monroe?'

His voice sharpened. 'I'm being perfectly serious, and I'd appreciate it if you would be as well. After all, you came here looking for something, didn't you? And so did I. Is it so unreasonable that someone else did as well?'

'But for what, Jeff?' Sally said gently. 'We came because we weren't happy at the circumstances of Miranda's death and hoped that maybe she had left a letter behind, or a diary ... anything that would have explained what Gregory Phillips was doing here with her. No one else could possibly have that interest, and even if they had, they'd hardly go about their search as last night's invaders did.'

He looked at her doubtfully. 'Maybe not. Now will you tell me again what happened when you went to get Mrs MacBride.'

Sally picked a wild pansy and a daisy to join the campion.

'She was upset, but not surprised. The cottage had been broken into the day after Miranda arrived.'

'So one theory goes bang. They weren't there looking for anything that would cast light on the drownings, and you said Miranda wouldn't let Mrs MacBride report it.'

'That's right, but there's nothing odd about that. Miranda wouldn't want the bother of it, especially if nothing had been taken.'

Suddenly he reached out his hand to hers. Sally, freezing, dropped her flowers to the ground.

'So we're left with her unknown friend.'

'*Two* unknown friends.' Sally said, her hand held in a firm clasp. 'The man Mrs MacBride saw her walking with and the man who came to the cottage. I think the latter is the most suspicious. The first could have been anyone, a tourist or a farmer. Anyone. But the second man was a Londoner. Mrs MacBride was quite sure about that, and *he* came *after* Miranda died. My money is on him.'

'My dear Sally, I always said you were an idiot but you don't have to go out of your way to prove it. The second man was myself.'

Sally stared open-mouthed. Jeff continued. 'I *did* tell you I'd been to the cottage and that the fearsome Mrs MacBride sent me off with a flea in my ear, didn't I? We're not looking for two men, Sally, only one, and I bet I know what his name is.'

'You do?'

'Of course. The mysterious Pete Mackay.'

'Then why did you want to walk out here to Octoford?'

'Why?' he said, his grip tightening for a second. 'To be alone with you of course.'

Sally felt her cheeks flame. 'Sarcasm doesn't suit you.'

'But I'm not being sarcastic.'

They stood motionless, facing each other with the seabirds soaring high above. Then he pulled her purposefully towards him, took her face in his hands, and kissed her. Against her will, she found herself returning his kiss, felt her whole body melt. Then, remembering all that had happened, she stiffened, and pushed him violently away.

'How *dare* you! You only apologized to me the other night!' She glared at him, the wind from the sea whipping her hair around her face. Angrily she brushed it away from her eyes, struggling to retain some dignity. Just as she was beginning to like him he had spoiled everything. Hot tears sprang to her eyes and she spun round hurriedly, stalking back down the windswept road. Of all the hateful, lowdown, mean, despicable . . .

He was beside her. Grabbing her arm, he swung her to face him, then, seeing the tears, he stopped, his expression one of stunned incredulity. Slowly he raised his hand and wiped her cheek while she bit her lip, choking with shame and humiliation, wishing herself a hundred miles away.

'Sally, for God's sake, what is it? What's the matter?'

'I resent . . .' Her voice floundered and she said with difficulty, 'I resent being made a fool of.'

'Being made a . . .' For the first time in his life, Jeff Roberts was speechless. They stared at each other silently, the waves thundering in the distance.

'It was a *kiss*, Sally,' he said eventually, sounding both perplexed and disconcerted.

'I know, but for the wrong reasons.' Her voice was still tearful and she was feeling more foolish with every passing minute. He gave her an odd look, still holding her firmly by both arms.

'Perhaps you'd better explain my reasons to me.'

She stood before him, the tears streaming down her face, unable to speak, too bemused herself to make much sense. If only she were not so affected by him! If only she could accept the fact that a kiss meant nothing to him. It was just a friendly reaction on his part, almost automatic. At the back of her mind, too, was a suspicion, very vague, but there . . . why should he have come to this island and to the cottage? Was he keeping something from her?

Forced to break the silence, she said at last, 'I know what you think of me, so I know the kiss didn't mean anything to you. But . . .' her voice faltered '. . . I can't play those sort of games . . .' She bent her head to hide a new onrush of tears. Oh, what was the matter with her?

'And what do I think?' he interrupted, his voice dangerously quiet. He put his hand beneath her chin, tilting it upwards so that she was forced to look directly at him. From the advantage of his six feet or more, he smiled down mockingly. For the first time she noticed that his eyes were golden brown and his hair deep auburn. She took a deep, steadying breath and said furiously, 'You're not amusing yourself with me for the lack of anything better to do!'

'But you *are* amusing.'

She stared at him, speechless at his rudeness, then spun round, marching through the long grass with as much dignity as she could muster. He caught up with her quickly, pulling her round to face him again, holding her close.

'Has no one ever told you that you are lovely?' he said, and then lowered his head and kissed her again. A long, warm kiss.

This time she did not struggle. She could not, for he was holding her so close she could scarcely breathe. He lifted his head a fraction away from hers and whispered: 'If you still find my behaviour unpleasant, you may go . . . but I'd rather you stayed.'

She stood immobile, hating herself, and hating him even more. He smiled disarmingly. 'Good. Now let's get one thing straight. I kissed you because I wanted to, have wanted to for quite a long time.'

A long time? Her thoughts ran. Then what about Miranda? Once more she wondered what their relationship was . . . before she could utter a word of protest, he kissed her again. She was aware of the gulls circling above their heads and the curlew crying and the grass brushing gently against her legs as the wind blew it. She was aware also of Jeff's reputation and that he was quite capable of flirting with her now so that she would help him find what he had come to Islay for. Perhaps he had loved Miranda; she longed to ask him but dare not. Despite herself, she was strangely happy with him. There was a new feeling in her body, a glow that was diffusing its warmth, making her soft and vulnerable. Eventually he let her go, and, her hand clasped firmly in his, said: 'Now let's do what we set out to do. Retrace Miranda's footsteps as far as we can.'

Subduing the questions she longed to ask, she said: 'Mrs MacBride saw her and the man walking across the grass from the road to the graveyard. She was in her sister's car and they were quite a distance away, but she was quite sure it was Miranda.'

'Well, one thing's for certain,' Jeff said grimly. 'They couldn't have been heading for anywhere else, except a long jump.'

She followed his gaze. Far out on the grass-covered headland high above the sea, crumbling walls encircled the exposed graveyard. There was no adjoining church, nothing but the waves pounding the cliffs below, and the open wind and the perpetual sea spray.

Sally's spine prickled at the loneliness and isolation and at the thought of the two figures who had walked along this same path not long ago.

'Come on,' Jeff said, jumping over the wall. 'Let's see what the attraction was.'

She shook her head in bewilderment. 'I can't imagine. Graveyards were my thing, not hers, and she wouldn't have come just for the walk.'

'What do you mean—graveyards are your thing?' Jeff asked, his arm around her waist as they strolled through the meadows of deep grass towards the sea. 'I've not fallen for a manic depressive, have I?'

She giggled. 'No, but I could never convince Miranda of that. I have this obsession with genealogy. I've done it as a hobby ever since I was a child. Once you start, it becomes compulsive. I trailed her all over the Kentish Weald a couple of years ago, searching the parish registers for the birth of a great, great grandfather. A mariner by profession but apparently one without roots. I never found proof of his birth anyway.'

'Sounds a riot,' Jeff said lightly. 'No wonder Miranda went away by herself this year.'

Sally's eyes clouded. 'I wish to goodness she hadn't. That was the start of it all. It didn't begin in Islay. It began in Turkey.'

Jeff was silent for a while, then he said: 'Didn't she speak about it at all?'

Sally shook her head. 'Not a thing. That's how I first knew something was wrong. You know what Miranda was like, bubbling over with enthusiasm about everything, a one-man band my father used to call her, but when she came back from Turkey she was quiet and withdrawn, no lavish descriptions of the Black Sea, no anecdotes, no funny stories about her drive home, nothing. I thought she was ill . . .'

'Or that it was a man.'

'And very rude you were when I asked you about that. You say *I* was standoffish . . .'

'At that time,' Jeff said firmly, 'there was no reason to think that Miranda was in trouble.'

'And now?'

He shrugged. 'I don't know, Sally. I honestly don't know.' He stared at the weatherbeaten headstones. 'Who was this guy in Turkey, the one with the Range Rover?'

'Tony Carpenter's brother. I asked her if he was attractive, and she said yes, he was, but that she wasn't in love with him and that he was more my type than hers.'

'And just what,' Jeff asked quietly, 'did she mean by that?'

'I've no idea,' Sally lied. 'But she never mentioned him again, and if he was like his brother I can't imagine he was likely to sweep Miranda off her feet. An effeminate slob was one of the kinder descriptions you used of him.'

'Said in the heat of the moment. I hardly know him. I'd never seen him before Gregory Phillips bought him to my party and I didn't speak to him then. He had Miranda pretty well cornered all evening if I remember correctly.'

'He *tried* to,' Sally said. 'That was the week before she left to do the Lee Domini pictures and she must have told him she was flying out to Turkey, I suppose he saw it as a heaven-sent chance to get his car brought back.'

'What was the brother's name?'

'I don't think I ever heard it mentioned. Or if I have, I've forgotten. Why?'

He frowned. 'I was just wondering if by any chance it was Pete.'

Sally shook her head. 'It was Pete Mackay not Carpenter. I don't think we need bother about him.'

'Perhaps not, but I think we should bother about Tony a bit more. After all, he was a friend of Gregory Phillips, he might be able to throw some light on to Phillips' relationship with Miranda.'

'Jeff,' Sally said hesitatingly, 'why did you once say to me that Miranda showed sense by not liking Gregory?'

'I don't remember saying that.'

'You did! You asked me if I was going to one of his parties and I said I wasn't and that Miranda wouldn't be either as she couldn't stand him, and you said, that's why I shouldn't worry about her, she showed sense.'

He paused for a second, considering, then he said flatly: 'Gregory Phillips was a louse.'

'Jeff!'

'I'm sorry, Sally, but you did ask. Do you remember Cora Bradley?'

'Yes. Isn't she in a sanatorium now? I was asking Miranda about her only a few weeks ago. I always found her rather sweet. What has she to do with Gregory?'

'Cora Bradley was Gregory Phillips' mistress.'

'Cora Bradley was . . .' Sally stared at him, round-eyed. 'But she was in her fifties, Jeff. Gregory was only twenty-six. You've surely made a mistake!'

'No mistake. She was also rich, soft and susceptible and Phillips played her for all he could.'

Sally didn't speak for a few minutes. She stared at the headstone before her, feeling sick and wondering for the first time what else she had been unaware of.

Jeff put his arm around her shoulders. 'Don't take it so badly, Sally. It's the kind of thing that happens and Cora was old enough to have known better. But you were right about her being sweet. She was a nice woman, generous and kind-hearted with everything going for her until she met Phillips. The ironic thing is that she would still have spent money on him even if he hadn't pretended to be in love with her. But that would have been honest and totally out of his character, so he lied, convinced her that the age difference didn't matter, that he wanted to marry her . . . Then he met another woman with money to be stupid with, and she was a bit younger, so it was good-bye to Cora in no uncertain terms.'

Jeff yanked a blade of grass savagely out of the ground. 'Saying good-bye was not enough for Phillips. He had to have the satisfaction of telling her what an old bag she was. He destroyed her. Cora Bradley was a fool, but she wasn't thick-skinned or egocentric. And she genuinely loved him, believed he loved her. By the time he'd finished with her, she was old and disillusioned. She can't face people now, and, God help her, she still loves him.'

'But that's . . . hideous,' Sally said brokenly.

'Isn't it just? Which is what I meant by Miranda showing sense in not liking him.'

'You mean Miranda *knew?*'

He nodded, and Sally stared out to sea. She had looked upon Miranda as a sister, believed there were no secrets between them and she was learning, minute by minute, that there was so much Miranda had not told her. Why? She asked herself. Why, Miranda?

Jeff said gently, 'She only kept things from you out of the best of intentions, Sally. Miranda had a hard shell and you haven't . . .'

'But don't you *see*,' she said shakily, 'other people besides you and Miranda knew what sort of man Gregory Phillips was, and now they'll think that he and Miranda were lovers!'

'Hey, steady on, Miranda's friends may well be puzzled at what Phillips was doing here with her, but one thing you can be sure of, they didn't believe that rubbish in the national press. And that's what we've come for, to find out why the hell he was here.'

'Well, one thing's for sure,' Sally said, kicking a tuft of grass viciously, 'Miranda hadn't asked him for the pleasure of his company.'

'I couldn't agree with you more, which brings me back to what I was saying; perhaps Tony Carpenter could throw some light on it.'

'Probably, but I don't know how to get in touch with him, do you?'

They strolled between the rows of overgrown graves and Jeff said, the laughter back in his voice, 'No, but it's no problem. I'll make a couple of phone calls when I get back to the hotel.' And taking Sally's hand, he went on: 'If I kiss you again do you promise to behave yourself?'

She took a deep breath. She simply had to know. 'Were you and Miranda having an affair?' She faltered.

He stared down at her, dark eyes clouded. 'Did Miranda tell you we were?'

She shook her head. 'No, it was just a . . . feeling.'

He paused as if about to say something, then changed his mind. 'No, we weren't.'

Then he drew her firmly towards him and kissed her again. She pushed the doubt to the back of her mind and then said, suddenly, breaking free from his embrace. 'Of course! I'd forgotten all about it! The evening Miranda left for Islay, we'd just reached the heath when Tony Carpenter drew up outside the flat. I told her we had a visitor and when she saw who it was, she just laughed and increased speed. He didn't leave a message, I looked specially when I got back, and he never rang. I wonder what he wanted?'

'Probably another favour,' Jeff said dryly, pulling her towards him again.

Later, when they had traversed every inch between the graves, and scoured the cliff face and coastline, they both admitted they were beaten.

'They must simply have come here as tourists,' Jeff said despairingly. 'If ancient burial grounds had no attraction for Miranda, they must have had for her friend. There's no other reason to come.'

Mutely Sally agreed with him.

'Let's get back to civilization and a hot meal, I've had enough of the Sherlock Holmes for one morning. I can make those phone calls as well, and this afternoon we'll have a trip round the island for the ubiquitous Pete Mackay.'

'Starting where?'

'At the post offices. We should be able to visit every one there is today and tomorrow. Come on.' And he was off, vaulting over the enclosing wall while she clambered laughingly after him, not noticing the large car that glided out from the side of the road, gathering speed quickly as it vanished in the direction of Port Charlotte.

Chapter Seven

'This morning was a wild goose chase, Sally,' Jeff said, as they walked briskly back towards the hotel. 'We should have started looking for Pete Mackay this morning not wasted it out here.'

'But I thought,' Sally said slyly, 'that you wanted to be alone with me?'

'So I did, my love, so I did,' he said, hugging her arm, 'but we've a long time ahead of us for that. At the moment we must concentrate exclusively on finding Pete Mackay. It's all we have to go on. Have you got Miranda's letter with you? I'd like to have another look at it.'

Obediently she rummaged in her shoulder-bag and handed it to him.

'*Dearest Sal*,' he read aloud. '*As usual I've reached the right decision too late, but at least I made it! I'm coming home tomorrow. I shall catch the early morning ferry and should be in London by seven or eight. If I don't make it, and I mean that quite literally, Pete Mackay will explain to you what's been happening these last few weeks. I can't be any clearer or you'll be in the same position as I am. Sorry I've been such a drag to you lately, but I tried to be too clever this time. Just one favour, Sal. Don't tell anyone I wrote to you, or where I've been or that you expect me back.*

We know each other so well that I don't have to put any more. I know you'll do what I want and remember, Sally, I love you and I'm sorry. Miranda.'

They stared at each other. 'What does she mean, she's been too clever?' Jeff asked.

'I wish I knew! Believe me, I've considered everything and I'm still no wiser. As you say, we can do nothing till we find Pete Mackay.'

'Come on then, I'm hungry and it's getting colder every minute.'

Hands held firmly, they began to jog-trot down the barren road.

'Jeff,' she said breathlessly after a little while, 'do you think it was one man or two who broke into An Cala? We keep saying he and then saying they . . .'

'It seems an awful lot of destruction for one man to accomplish in the short time you were away. There were probably two of them. Don't worry, Sally, we'll find out.'

'Yes.'

Jeff squeezed her hand. 'You're still determined to go on staying there? You could move into the hotel, they've room for you.'

'I don't think so,' said Sally in a voice that sounded braver than she felt. 'They've overhauled the cottage twice now, they won't do it a third time.'

A shadow passed over his face and she pressed his hand.

'I'll be all right, Jeff,' she said and smiled confidently. 'Whatever they're looking for isn't in the cottage, and I want to stay there.'

'You're only staying there because I happen to agree with you. If I thought for one minute there was any danger you'd move into the hotel whether you wanted to or not!'

Sally laughed.

'Never mind you laughing, girl. I mean it,' said Jeff. 'When I say it's time to pack your bags and head home, you do as you're told, understand?'

'We'll cross that bridge when we come to it,' she said with a smile.

'I'm not joking, Sally. There's something in that letter you seem to have overlooked.'

At the tone of his voice the smile vanished from her lips. She said anxiously, 'What do you mean?'

"I can't explain any clearer or you'll be in the same position as I am," he quoted. 'If you do find what the intruders were searching An Cala for, it sounds to me as if you'd have to leave Islay pretty

speedily. I think that's what happened to Miranda. She didn't leave speedily enough.'

'Dear God,' said Sally, standing motionless in the centre of the road, the colour draining from her face. 'Do you really think she was murdered, and Gregory Phillips too?'

'I do. Everything points to it. The fact that she was a strong swimmer who had known the bay since she was a child, the letter, the cottage being broken into, it all adds up.' His face was grim. 'The more I think about it, the more convinced I am. But why . . .?' The question hung in the air, puzzling and unanswerable.

Sally said in a tight voice, 'I think I've known it all along, but it seemed so impossible . . . so . . .'

He bent his head and kissed her. 'Brooding on it won't help Miranda and it won't help us. Action is what is needed, and we'll get plenty of that this afternoon. Come on, I can see the hotel from here. The sooner we have lunch the sooner we can make a start.'

They hurried past the stout, pink-walled masonry of Port Charlotte's outlying cottages and into the welcoming warmth of the hotel dining-room.

'An' did you have a nice mornin'?' the little waitress asked, as she placed steaming bowls of soup in front of them. 'You must be sure to visit the Cross before you go home. Mr and Mrs Rees'—she nodded in the direction of the stoutly-booted couple at the corner table—'they went yesterday.'

'The Cross?' Jeff asked.

'Why, of course,' she exclaimed, obviously taken aback by his ignorance. 'It's ever so old. *Everyone* goes to see it.'

'And whereabouts is it?' Jeff asked, giving her the full benefit of a smile.

She blushed. 'Away over at Kildalton.'

Sally looked up sharply. 'Kildalton?'

'Aye, there's just the church there and the Cross. You canna miss it.'

'Kildalton,' Sally said to Jeff. 'I'm sure that's where Mrs MacBride said Miranda had been the day she arrived back to find the cottage broken into. It was Kildalton or Kilcholden or something like that.'

'Oh aye,' the young waitress interrupted cheerfully. 'There's Kildalton, Kilchiaron, Kilchoman, Kilmeny, Kilnave, Kilarrow . . .'

Jeff grinned at Sally. 'And you're not sure which it was?'

'No, but I'll ask Mrs MacBride tonight. I want to go everywhere I know Miranda went.'

'Well, if it's as productive as this morning's jaunt, good luck to you,' Jeff said dryly. 'I'll stay in the bar!'

'Celtic,' said a loud voice to the right of them. 'One of the finest pieces of Celtic workmanship to be found anywhere in the world.' Mr Rees leant across confidentially. 'Even finer than the Ionian Cross, though not everyone would agree with me. Magnificent example of fourteenth-century art at its best. There are two more of the same period, not as good but still remarkable. One is at Kilchoman and the other at Kilnave. Well worth visiting, *well* worth visiting.'

His ruddy face beamed at them over his thick, knitted roll-necked sweater. 'As for Standing Stones . . .' He whistled expressively. 'As thick on the ground as the sheep. Why, only this morning I saw one of the most interesting stone circles I've ever laid eyes on. Just west of the Portnahaven Kilchiaron road. Stonehenge, that's all most people think about, but here on Islay there's a wealth of Druidic remains, a wealth.' He clasped his hands between his knees, saying earnestly, 'Visit Kildalton first, and then search out some Standing Stones. I'll lend you my book, most of them are difficult to locate.' He handed Jeff a well-thumbed, leather-bound volume. 'Everything you want to know in there, everything.' He raised a hand to silence Jeff's protests.

'No, I insist. You can let me have it back tomorrow at dinner. I can see you're interested and it's my pleasure, my pleasure entirely.'

With another beam he pushed his chair back. 'Nice to meet people with enthusiasm, very nice.' Oozing goodwill, he escorted Mrs Rees out into the lounge, speculating loudly on the number of megalithic graves they would be able to locate before they returned home.

Jeff grinned. 'There goes one man who is enjoying his holiday.'

'If all I had on my mind was Druidic remains and

fourteenth-century crosses, I'd be happy as well. Let's hurry our lunch and get on with the task of finding Pete Mackay.'

'Okay. I'll leave the phone calls till tonight. I don't expect I'd find many people at home this time of day anyway. How shall we do it, separately or together?'

'It would be quicker separately,' Sally said, a trifle doubtfully.

'But friendlier together. To hell with efficiency. We'll just move extra fast.'

She laughed. 'Where shall we start?'

'Here, of course, and then round the bay.' He cleared half of the table and spread out a large map of the island, tracing the road with his finger as he spoke. 'Bruichladdich may have a post office and Bridgend, any place s in between we'll just have to keep an eye out. Then from Bridgend we'll go to Bowmore then slice across the mainland to Port Ellen and follow the coast road from there to Lagavulin and Kildalton. The road peters out soon after that so we'll have to backtrack to Port Ellen and take the secondary road from there to Bridgend again, and then across to the far side of the island and Port Askaig. If we have no success we'll have to look at the electoral rolls . . .'

'*Phone books!*' Sally exclaimed triumphantly.

Jeff shook his head in mock despair. 'I've already done that, with no luck. Come on, let's make tracks.'

The afternoon sun was strong and the light clear and pure as they drove out of Port Charlotte. To the right of them the waters of Loch Indaal glistened aquamarine and turquoise, the waves breaking gently over the moss-covered rocks that pierced the sea.

Jeff increased speed, sweeping past a couple of newly-built cottages with only the seagulls for company, and continuing down the wide curve that led to the head of the loch. Here the landscape changed, the steep banks that edged the road giving way to a flat expanse of lush green grass with sheep grazing and ignoring the intrusion of a bright orange tent pitched amongst their midst, the wind filling it till it looked as though it would snap its guy ropes and soar out to sea. Now there were no houses, only an occasional farm, and Bowmore, neat and tidy, looking like a toy-town on the far side of the loch. The shore was deep in smooth, rounded pebbles, with half a dozen cows incongruously picking their way amongst them, flicking their tails idly and apparently enjoying the salt-laden air. They passed a turning for Coullabus and Sally raised an enquiring brow.

'Later, Sally. Let's try the larger villages first.'

As they neared Bridgend, the scenery softened. A small group of trees flanked the road, petered out, then thickened into cool, dim woodland, the pebbled shore giving way to a flat green plain of waving rushes. A high cultivated hedge replaced the trees, leading them away from the sea and into a belt of deep woodland that surrounded Bridgend.

Jeff drew to a halt outside the Bridgend Hotel, which looked more like a Kentish village pub with its eaves over the doors and ivy-clad, whitewashed walls.

'There's no point in you getting out of the car, Sally. All of Bridgend is here.' He gestured to the bank and the handful of houses and stray shop. 'It won't take a minute.'

He slammed the door behind him and sprinted across the narrow road. Five minutes later he was back, shaking his head. 'Nothing doing, Sally. Bowmore next stop.'

'That's the largest place on the island, isn't it? Perhaps we'll have more luck there, and besides the post office, they'll have the council offices and everything.'

'We'll give them a try later, if the post office fails.'

They sped out from Bridgend's shelter of trees into open country, following the coast road to Bowmore. The tide was out and had left large, landlocked pools of water enticingly full of shells and brilliant sea anemones, the sun sparkling on their still surfaces as on a mirror.

Sally suppressed a longing sigh, trying to ignore them and the mass of wild flowers that bobbed their heads luringly in the hedgerows in a riot of vivid colour. Rich farmland with herds of well-fed cows bordered the road, bringing them into Bowmore with its rows of two-toned houses and busy main square.

Jeff parked beside the other cars and opened the door for her.

To the right, the street ran for fifty yards or so, flanked by the hotel, a jeweller's, a baker's, two sprucely-kept cottages and an expensive-looking souvenir shop, and ending abruptly at a small, stone jetty and a cluster of boats. To the left, the road climbed steeply, culminating in a round, Victorian church that Sally vaguely remembered reading about. Round, if she remembered rightly, to allow the devil no place to hide in. The other road that sliced the square had its fair share of shops and houses with singing yellow doors and neatly-curtained windows. She took Jeff's hand and walked with him down the street in search of the post office.

'I'm afraid I'll not be knowin'.' The elderly man in charge peered at them over his spectacles. 'Try Mrs Curtis next door, yon's the one that will know if anyone does. The name isn't familiar, though I believe there is a Patrick Mackay away at Bruichladdich.'

'Ach, but I'd be tellin' you a lie if I said there was,' Mrs Curtis said unhelpfully. 'I'm thinkin' you've a hard job ahead of you, an' is it important then?'

In answer to their nodded affirmations she pursed her lips, concentrating hard. 'There's a lot of Mackays in Islay, but a Pete ... Now Mr MacDonald, bein' who he is and workin' in the post office, he should have known. As for myself I can only think of the Mackay away at Kiells an' he must be ninety if he's a day, but his name is Peter. Ach, but he'll not be the one you're searchin' for ... why, he's been bed-ridden since last Hogmanay.' She paused. 'An' then there's Pete Mackay of Port Ellen but he's a sailor an' not at home, I'm thinkin'.' With genuine regret she shook her head. 'The only other is wee Pete Mackay at Ballygrant an' he is only eight years old.'

'Well, thank you very much for trying to help us,' Jeff said. 'If you do remember anyone by that name I'm staying at the hotel in Port Charlotte and I'd be very grateful if you'd give me a ring.'

'Ach, surely,' Mrs Curtis said affably. 'But I'm thinkin' it will take you a wee bitty longer to find him.'

'Where now?' Sally asked as they strolled back to the car.

'Port Ellen. Perhaps Pete Mackay the sailor is at home. He sounds a little more likely than the other two, and we may find some other

Pete Mackays. Don't look so dispirited, Sally, we've a lot of places to visit yet.'

'Yes,' she agreed. 'And like Mrs Curtis said, "It's going to take us a wee bitty longer."'

They drove up the steep main street and past the church into a hedged lane green with wild grass and flowers. Small groups of conifers crowded the banks of a tumbling stream and then they were out across the flat moorland.

Sally leant back, gazing rapturously at the vast expanse of sea and the clouds scudding over the purple heather and the gorse, golden and bright, with only the curlews and an occasional sheep to disturb the stillness. Wild bog cotton waved silver heads in the breeze and in the distance lay the giant curve of Laggan Bay with the Atlantic breakers thundering on to a deserted shore. Miranda had been right when she had said that Sally would love it. Even under the present circumstances Islay was casting its spell. She gazed over at the far-away hills, blue behind a faint veil of mist … Miranda had always known her so well … what she would like … what she would do … *We know each other so well that I don't have to put any more. I know you'll do what I want!…*

What was it that Miranda would have expected her to do? Come here certainly, but what then? How did Miranda expect her to find Pete Mackay? Surely not like this. There had to be an easier way, so obvious that she hadn't even thought of it …*I know you'll do what I want* … But what was it? What on *earth* was it?

Port Ellen proved to be a disappointment. Pete Mackay the sailor had not been home for the last six months and the young girl in the post office could give them no help. Determinedly they set off for Lagavulin, with the breath-taking view of a sparkling blue sea and a coastline of craggy creeks and islets as compensation. Trees heavy with scarlet berries overhung the road and minutes later they were curving among the pristine white cottages of Lagavulin village.

Every window-sill was spilling over with flowers, tubs massed with geraniums and honeysuckle and vivid red begonias stood by the doorways and the air was heavy with the hum of bees. But no one had heard of Pete Mackay.

By the time they'd reached Kidalton, only to be told the same thing there, they had neither the wish nor inclination to break off their search for a view of the Cross. Instead, they retraced the road as far as Port Ellen to Bridgend. The wind had dropped and the weather was perfect, with a hot sun burning down on to wild moorland that stretched as far as the eye could see, and the gaunt Paps of Jura rising magnificently in the distance. Richly coloured bracken enveloped the low stone walls that edged the narrow road, and dandelions defiantly thrust their golden heads above the bracken's choking mass.

In the distance Sally could see a pile of neatly stacked peats, and then, as they drew nearer, the grey stone of a building and the tell-tale flash of a red postbox set into the wall. She nudged Jeff.

'There's a post office there. Should we stop?'

'And a signpost.'

He slowed down. The house was sturdily built, half-hidden by the high stacks of drying peats, and through one window could be seen a counter backed by shelves of groceries. A yard or so beyond it a track led off the road, winding over the steep moorland and into the hills and signposted Sullom.

'I can't imagine they get much custom,' Jeff said, as they slammed the car doors behind. 'But we'll give it a try, we may be lucky.'

Sally wasn't so hopeful. 'I just can't believe that Miranda would say to get in touch with someone who was so hard to find! It makes as little sense as everything else. She surely can't have expected me to have to search every acre of Islay to find him!'

'Well, of course, if you've any *better* ideas,' Jeff said, opening the wooden door and stepping into a room crammed from floor to ceiling with tinned foods, cereals, sacks of potatoes, old-fashioned jars of sweets, 'please let me know!'

'Don't be so touchy. It's just that I'm sure there's something we've overlooked. Something staring us in the face.'

A sharp-faced woman, easily as tall as Jeff, stared at them from behind a solid counter of polished wood. She had a dark brown overall wrapped tightly around her with the sleeves rolled up, and she didn't look too pleased at being disturbed from what she was doing. The floor was wet and in one hand she still held the handle of her mop while a bucket of soapy water steamed at her feet.

Jeff bought a packet of biscuits and a box of chocolates and said, 'Do you know of anyone by the name of Pete Mackay living hereabouts?'

Her head was bent over the drawer where her change was kept, and she didn't look up as she said, 'An' is he a friend of yours?'

'A friend of a friend. We promised we'd look him up.'

'An' you're not knowin' where it is he's livin'?'

'I'm afraid not. Do you know anyone of that name?'

The woman pushed the coins across the counter with slow deliberation.

'I'm afraid not. Mackay's a common enough name, but I'm thinkin' you'd need to get his address from your friend.'

Jeff pocketed his change. 'Yes, I think you're right. Thanks anyway. Good-bye.'

The woman didn't bother to reply, she simply reached out for her mop. Compared with the standard of courtesy usually shown by the islanders, her behaviour was rude and Sally turned at the doorway to say good-bye again, determined to show friendliness.

The mop lay forgotten against the wall, and she was staring after them so malevolently through half-closed eyes that Sally's words faltered on her lips and she ran after Jeff, letting the door slam behind her.

'Whew, I'm glad that's not *my* local shop,' she said as she climbed into the car beside Jeff.

'We interrupted her, that's all,' Jeff said comfortably, handing her the chocolates.

'But if you saw the look she gave us as we left . . .'

'Your imagination,' Jeff said indulgently. 'Forget her.'

Chapter Eight

The moorland grew hillier and was relieved by plantations of young fir trees and masses of yellow broom. Sally sighed.

'I really don't think we're getting anywhere, Jeff.'

He squeezed her hand. 'Maybe not, but it will do no harm to finish what we set out to do. I'll phone London when we get back to the hotel and try and get hold of Tony Carpenter. Cheer up, Sally, it's only our first day; we can't expect miracles.'

'But if Miranda told me to see Pete Mackay, she must have assumed I would find him easily enough,' Sally said doggedly. 'All this searching just doesn't seem right.'

'As I said before, if you can think of anything else, just tell me. This isn't the most sensible thing I've ever done in my life, but it's there in black and white. *If anything happens to me, Pete Mackay will explain.*'

'What,' Sally asked tentatively after a little while, 'if something happened to Pete Mackay as well?'

Jeff was silent for a moment, negotiating a couple of wandering cows. 'Even if it had, *someone* must still have heard of him. No, I think he's alive and well.'

'And living in Islay?'

'Or London.'

'London!' Sally exclaimed, sitting bolt upright.

'Could be,' Jeff said blandly. 'But if it is, it won't be quite like looking for a needle in a haystack. The odds are that someone else who knew Miranda also knows Pete Mackay. We'll simply ask the people Miranda knew if they've heard of him.'

Sally groaned. 'But that could take *ages*.'

'Exactly. Which is why we'll have it done professionally ...'

'Professionally? You mean, with a private detective?'

'Coupled with the police. We might get them interested, you never know.'

Sally stared glumly out of the window. 'It has to be easier than this, Jeff. There's something we've overlooked, something obvious.'

'Well, you just think of it and give me a shout,' Jeff said, as the dim green of Bridgend's woods closed above them for a second time.

'You don't think ...' She hesitated. 'You don't think it's got anything to do with the book?'

Jeff took the Port Askaig road and shook his head. 'As far as I'm concerned, Sally, the book doesn't figure anywhere. Someone broke into An Cala looking for something. They didn't find what they wanted, at least we're *presuming* they didn't, but the book caught their eye and they took it. As simple as that.'

'And if they did find what they broke in for?'

Jeff shrugged. 'We still want to find Pete Mackay, it doesn't alter that.'

Four hours later they were still no nearer their objective. Port Askaig had been a waste of time, and so had all the other innumerable villages and hamlets and isolated shops that they had stopped at. As far as Islay was concerned, Pete Mackay did not exist.

When finally they returned to the hotel, Sally sank down wearily on to one of the lounge chairs. 'I shall be asking for that wretched man in my sleep tonight,' she said wearily.

'*You* will!' Jeff said feelingly. 'I'm the one who did all the work, and there's more to do. You stay here and have a rest, while I phone London.'

She closed her eyes, easing her tired feet out of her shoes, while Jeff disappeared in the direction of the telephone. From the cocktail bar came the distant sound of Mr Rees elaborating to an unseen audience on the romance of Islay, of the Vikings, of the Kingdom of the Isles ... of the Clan Donal ...

When she woke up Jeff was sitting opposite her, a large drink in one hand and an unfathomable expression in his eyes. He smiled and the look vanished, so that Sally was no longer sure if it had been there or if it had been her imagination, but the nagging doubt in her mind as to Jeff's sincerity stirred again. He had reached the top of his profession by a combination of talent and ruthlessness. Was he being ruthless now? Was it too much of a coincidence that here, where she could perhaps be of use to him, he was attentive, when in London he had virtually ignored her?

'Come on, Sleeping Beauty, dinner is served.'

'Goodness, is it that late? I was half-listening to Mr Rees and I fell asleep.'

'Don't tell him that or you'll hurt his feelings. He's still going strong. Listen.'

'The great Somerled inherited the Celtic kingdom of Argyll from his father and then proceeded to drive the Norse out of Argyll and the Isles. Fascinating story, utterly fascinating. The sea battle that clinched it . . .'

They smiled at each other and Jeff leant forward to kiss her gently before they went into the dining-room and a dinner of stuffed pork flamed in whisky. As the plates were taken away, to be replaced by fresh fruit and cream, Jeff said: 'I'm leaving tomorrow morning for London.'

Sally's spoon remained motionless in mid-air. 'I forgot all about the telephone calls. What happened?'

'I got Tony Carpenter's number from Gregory Phillips' sister. He said Gregory and Miranda had been having an affair for three or four months . . .'

'He's a liar!'

'Steady on, Sally. Let me finish. He also said there were some things of Miranda's still at Gregory's flat, clothes and a briefcase, and as he intends moving in there, would I kindly remove them.'

'And you think . . .'

'It's a chance, Sally. I want to get down there and see what's in the briefcase before anyone else does.'

'But why on earth should any of Miranda's things be at Gregory's flat?'

62

His face expressionless, Jeff said, 'I've no idea, but I want to find out.'

'But Miranda wouldn't have looked twice at Gregory Phillips,' Sally declared flatly.

'Then why are her things there?' Jeff asked.

'Jeff Roberts, I hope you don't think I've had affairs with everyone I've happened to leave any of my belongings with, otherwise the list would be as long as your arm! Miranda was always leaving her things behind her. You, of all people, should know that.'

He grinned. 'You're very probably right. As for belongings, I'll leave all mine here. I should be back the day after tomorrow if I can get on a sleeper to Stirling.'

'Perhaps, if there's something in the briefcase, there'll be no need for you to come back at all.'

'There'll be a need all right.' He covered her hand with his. 'We have some appointments to keep.'

She stared at him blankly.

'With the Kidalton Cross, and that gorgeous beach we saw this morning, and a walk up the slopes of Ben Tartaville . . .'

Sally laughed. 'You're quite right. I won't be able to rest till I find out the full story of Somerled and make Mr Rees happy by looking at his Standing Stones or Druidic circles or whatever it is he's so anxious we look at.'

'What will you do tomorrow?'

'Find Pete Mackay all by myself and then spend the rest of the day lounging in the sun.'

'Okay, Miss Clever, but just remember: *lock the cottage door when you go to bed.*'

She looked at him steadily, and then said with a little smile, 'But if you're in London, Jeff, I shall be quite safe!'

'Never mind the witticisms, just remember to do it. And, Sally . . .'

'Yes?'

'Oh well, never mind for the moment. But just take care of yourself. Now, promise.'

The look in his eyes subdued all her doubts—at least momentarily.

'Jeff . . .' but the question she was going to ask went unspoken.

'And how did you get on then?' Mr Rees, beaming good-naturedly and blissfully unaware of what he was interrupting, laid a hand on Jeff's shoulder.

'Find the circle of Standing Stones, did you?'

'I'm afraid not,' Jeff said, turning to face him. 'We've been rather busy today, but we'll certainly visit the Cross before we leave.'

'Keep the book then,' Mr Rees said generously. 'We're here for another week, you can give it back to me before you go.'

'That's very good of you, but you'll want it yourself, surely?'

'No, no,' Mr Rees said, rocking back on his heels. 'That book only goes up to 800 AD. Marvellous for the Druidic remains, indispensable. There's a lovely little Sun Circle on the Ardnave Peninsula . . . now, what was the grid reference?' He flicked hastily through the book Jeff had brought with him to return and laid it on the table. 'Here it is, Number 273734. There are still fourteen stones standing upright and it wasn't found till 1961! I think that's remarkable, that such historic treasures should be virtually ignored . . . goodness only knows how many more Islay is hiding.'

'You mean it just wasn't recognized for what it was?' Jeff asked.

'Probably, probably, but this one in particular isn't easy to find, it's completely obscured by a low cliff. Anyone standing on higher ground would miss it completely. It has to be approached along the shoreline, and very rocky it is too. But well worth the trouble, well worth the trouble.'

'What were these circles used for, Mr Rees?' Sally asked, helping herself to some more of the local cheese.

'There you have me,' he said, running his hand over his chin. 'Theories abound, but the truth? All I can say is that they were places of worship, Temples of the Sun. To the ancient Celt the sun was the father of Man and the druids were the priests. It was a universal religion, Miss Craig. Look at the circles to be found in England and Wales and Ireland, and further afield under the ancient city of Heliopolis, there are traces of a sun circle. They've been found all over the world. May Day and Hallowe'en were the dates when their most important rituals were carried out, traces of which still linger in our society today. It's a fascinating subject, absolutely fascinating. We spent all last week searching out all we could and now I want to visit sites that relate to more modern history, to the Clan Donald and the Lordship of the Isles ... So you can keep the book till we leave ...'

'Perhaps you could do me a favour?' Jeff said, carefully avoiding Sally's eyes. 'Unfortunately I have to make a quick visit to London in the morning on business, and Miss Craig will be left by herself for a couple of days. She's very interested in learning more about Islay's history, and if you could ...'

'Say no more, it would be my pleasure entirely.' His cherry cheeks positively glowed as he smiled broadly across at Sally. 'I'm not an authority, Miss Craig, but I've read a lot. Angela gets tired of all my tramping about sometimes, she's refused point blank to come to Dunyveg any more with me. I've been there every day so far ...'

'Dunyveg?'

'The ruined castle of the Lords of the Isles.' He took a deep breath. 'It stands on a rocky promontory near Kildalton and ...'

Jeff tapped his arm lightly. 'I think Mrs Rees is waiting for you.'

Mrs Rees, sitting by herself at the far side of the room, had the expression of a woman well used to waiting and quite resigned to it, but Mr Rees took the hint.

'I'll keep a look out for you tomorrow, Miss Craig. Let's hope the weather stays fine. Perhaps I could show you Dunyveg if it does.'

'Yes,' Sally said, smiling. 'That would be lovely.'

'Good ... good ... look forward to it.'

Four yards later he was deep in conversation with another guest, and Mrs Rees continued to sit by herself, sensibly eating her dinner and not waiting for her errant husband to join her.

'And will you?' Jeff asked.

'Go to Dunyveg? If I have the time. What I want to do first is see Mrs MacBride and ask her where it was Miranda had said she'd been. Then I think I'll go wherever it was and have a look round.'

'Remembering Octoford, I'm nearly glad I'll be in London,' Jeff said feelingly.

'And I might even go back to that shop.'

'Shop?' Jeff asked. 'What shop?'

'Where you bought the biscuits and chocolates.'

'Sally, I've bought so many unnecessary articles today from so many different shops that I haven't the faintest idea which one you mean.'

'The little shop all by itself in the wilds, next to the signpost for Sullom.'

'Would it be rude of me to ask what for?'

Sally shrugged. 'Feminine intuition. Nothing else.'

He shook his head in despair. 'You really are the silliest . . .'

'I know, I know, stupidest girl you've ever met . . .'

'But very lovely all the same . . . and very lovable too. But don't go wasting your time calling back there. If I remember rightly, that was the woman who upset you when we left.'

'That,' Sally said patiently, 'is the reason I thought I'd go back. She had no reason to look at us like that, unless . . .'

'Not everyone appreciates tourists infiltrating their seclusion, Sally. Take my advice and give her a wide berth. Dunyveg with Mr Rees will be much more pleasant.'

'Yes,' Sally said absently, but she did not change her mind about the shop.

'And now,' Jeff said, mistakenly thinking his advice had been taken, 'let's go for a walk on the beach. It's too nice an evening to spend inside.'

They carried their shoes, walking hand in hand along the firm, pale sand, the incoming waves breaking into surging foam as they slid over their feet. It was very quiet and then Jeff said, 'We'll come to Islay for our honeymoon, shall we?' Sally stopped abruptly, hardly able to speak for the constriction in her throat, and looked at him in wide-eyed astonishment. 'But, but . . .' she stammered.

Jeff laughed and swept her into his arms. 'I know, I know. So far I haven't asked for your hand, haven't said I love you. But I do. Oh, I do.'

He felt her tremble in his arms and his arms tightened about her. 'Oh, you,' he whispered. 'There is no other girl like you. Well, shall we come to Islay for our honeymoon?'

'Are you sure?' was all she could say, blinking away her tears.

'What a damned fool question! Of course I am.' And he kissed her in a manner that left little doubt.

Afterwards he said a little unsteadily, 'And you, Sally? Are you sure? It's not so long since you were accusing me of bullying and shouting . . .' He put a hand under her chin, tilting her face upwards.

'Quite, quite sure,' she said fervently. And again: 'Quite sure.'

His cheek moved against her hair and he said, 'I didn't realize till now how alone I've been.' And Sally, remembering what Miranda had said about his childhood and the brusque, self-sufficient exterior that he always presented, recognized for the first time how thick the veneer had been. She put her arms round him and held him close, her heart beating so hard that it almost hurt.

The sun was setting now, and the light bathing the stark outline of the hills was an ethereal gold, fingers of vermilion and amber clawed the sky, while beneath them the sea was as smooth as glass, luminous in the reflected glory. Behind were sand dunes, spiky with coarse sea grass and greener banks, thick with harebells and hedge-parsley and riddled with rabbit holes. A cool breeze from the hills carried with it the tang of drying peats and the faint tinkling of a freshwater stream running down to the shore. As they approached the arm of the bay, they could see the waves breaking against the black bases of the cliff and the night clouds gathering, tinged a deep rosy-pink from the sinking sun, and beginning to drift inland. There was no sound, except for the gentle lap water and the fluttering moths.

All was serene and beautiful, and peaceful. The last lull before the storm.

Chapter Nine

Jeff left Port Askaig on the first ferry the next day. Sally stood on the quayside, her heavy cardigan wrapped warmly around her, waiting until he was lost to view. It was cold and damp and there was a faint mist rolling in from the sea. Despondently she turned and walked across to her car, trying to overcome the sudden loneliness that she felt. She tried to tell herself that Jeff would be back tomorrow night or the day after, there was really no need to feel so bereft, but the hours until his return stretched out endlessly before her and she gripped the door handle of the car, staring out after the small boat as it sailed out of the Sound of Islay and into the open Atlantic. She had to fill in the hours somehow. If she could find Pete Mackay all by herself before he came back . . .

She pressed her foot on the accelerator, and climbed the steep hill out of Port Askaig. When she came to Bridgend she paused. Across the bay Port Charlotte's cottages huddled the shore, and no doubt Mr Rees would be in the hotel and only too keen to take her sight-seeing . . . to the left was the secondary road to Port Ellen . . . and the shop at the turn-off for Sullom. Without a backward glance she swung the wheel hard left, speeding down the straight road across the moors.

There was a strong breeze from the sea and Sally wound down the car window. Her spirits lifted as the air stung her cheeks and she found herself enjoying the smell of peat and heather; even the desolation that stretched out on either side held a strange beauty.

In the few minutes it took to reach the Sullom signpost and the white track that led into the hills, Sally felt on top of the world, despite the fact that Jeff was heading hundreds of miles away from her. He had said he loved her, hadn't he? That should make her the happiest girl in the world. She parked the car and humming to herself she slung her bag on to her shoulder and strolled across the loose pebbles and into the shop. At the sound of the door opening, the woman inside turned, her lips tightening at the sight of Sally.

It seemed even darker and more crowded inside the shop than it had the previous day. Sally smiled determinedly as she skirted the sacks of wheat and potatoes.

'I'm sorry to bother you again,' she said, with as much friendliness as possible. 'But I wondered if you had remembered anyone by the name of Pete Mackay.'

'You asked me that yesterday an' I said no.'

'I know,' Sally said apologetically. 'But I thought I'd call by, just in case you'd remembered after we'd gone. It's terribly important.'

'In trouble, is he?'

'Good heavens no!' Sally exclaimed, genuinely startled.

The woman's face, which had remained carefully shuttered, relaxed slightly. She took a step forward, gazing speculatively at Sally through narrowed eyes.

'You know him, don't you?' Sally asked quietly.

'Ach, that's my affair. Happen he'd not be pleased at me for sending strangers along.'

'But he'll *want* to see me,' Sally said desperately. 'It's if you don't tell me where I can find him that he'll be angry.'

They stared at each other and then the woman shrugged, wiping her large hands on the rough apron that she wore, as if ridding herself of the whole affair.

'Don't blame me if you get no welcome. The Mackays don't like strangers pokin' around their farm. The only one I ever see is the girl . . .'

'Where is the farm?'

'Way past Sullom out in the hills. It's rough goin'. Your car will not get you all the way . . .'

With a hurried and grateful thank you, Sally practically ran out of the shop. That this Pete Mackay was the one they wanted she

69

hadn't a shadow of doubt. Gleefully she started the car and headed down the narrow track, past the handful of crofts that were Sullom, towards the misty blue hills of inner Islay, imagining the disbelief on Jeff's face when he returned.

On either side of her the moors stretched out in a vast expanse of purples and browns, barren of trees but rich in tumbling streams that rushed over rocky beds, sparkling and clear, the precious water that enabled the island's distilleries to make their malts. For a brief second she caught the sight of antlers fretting the distant sky-line and gasped with pleasure, then they were gone, and there was only the wide, wind-blown landscape and a crumbling stone wall, long since fallen into disrepair, edging the track that grew-rapidly rougher and more overgrown.

Ten minutes later the way was barred by a large metal gate, but beyond it the track, now only a shadow on the turf, continued winding higher. With difficulty Sally slipped the catch, swinging the gate open, then she drove the car through, getting out once more in order to close it. The damp that had been in the air since early morning had increased to a light drizzle and the clouds blowing in from the sea were grey and heavy. She shivered, running quickly back to the car, trying to ignore the oppressive desolation. The track became wilder, over-grown with grass and thistles, and she was already climbing the lower slopes of the hills. Ahead of her were ridge after ridge of them, sweeping down into shallow cups and hollows where occasional bushes grew tenaciously in the inhospitable ground.

A few yards later and the barely discernible track petered out altogether. Sally pulled on the handbrake and gazed around. In front and to the left and the right were the seemingly endless hills, and behind her the fells curved down to the vast expanse of peat and bog. She turned the key in the ignition and tried to move forwards but the ground was too rough and steep, and she knew that if she persevered she would damage the car. Resignedly she reached into the back seat for her coat: she would walk for ten minutes, that was all, and if there were still no sign of the Mackay farm by then she would go back to Port Charlotte and wait until Jeff returned.

The hills swept down on either side, forming a narrow gully, and Sally headed towards it. The heather was damp and springy beneath her feet, then, just as she was about to turn back, she rounded a bluff, and before her, cupped in a hollow, lay the Mackay farm. A small, squat cottage nestled beside larger, straggling outbuildings, vividly white against the bracken-covered hills, and as she paused to get a better look at it, she heard the unmistakable lowing of cattle floating towards her on the wind. She thrust her hands deeper into her pockets and quickened her pace downwards.

The gate to the farm was stiff and heavy and crimson with rust. Sally put her shoulder to it, and managed to open it wide enough to squeeze through. It clanged to noisily behind her, the sound reverberating in the still air, but no one emerged from the farm, no smoke rose from the chimney and its whole appearance was one of neglect and desolation, with no sign of life save for the smell of the animals and the mountains of straw piled in the byre.

With growing disquiet she knocked on the door. She heard the murmur of voices and out of the corner of her eye Sally saw a curtain twitch back. And then nothing, no sound at all. Taking a deep breath, she knocked again, this time louder. Still nothing, then, as her hand rose for the third time, the door swung open and a young girl faced her, staring inquisitively with shadowed eyes. Her hair was a thick tangle of chestnut and she wore a pair of cumbersome Wellington boots and a shapeless overall. She continued to stare at Sally, saying nothing.

'Could I . . . is . . .' For a moment Sally faltered, then she took a deep breath and said firmly, 'Could I speak to Pete Mackay, please?'

Slowly the girl's eyes travelled from Sally's muddy shoes to her clothes and finally to her face and hair. Wondering if perhaps the girl only spoke Gaelic, Sally tried again, this time slower.

'Could I speak to Pete Mackay, please?'

Heavy footsteps sounded from the depths of the cottage, and then the door was wrenched from the girl's hand by a powerfully built man of perhaps forty, with the same unkept appearance as the girl, and dark, sullen eyes.

'What the hell do you want? This is private property. Private, you understand?'

'I'd like to speak to Pete Mackay,' Sally said uncertainly.

'*I'm* Pete Mackay. What the devil do you want with me?'

The girl had inched back and was peering round the edge of the door, while he straddled the threshold, his eyes narrowing as he glared down at her.

Sally, rapidly wishing she had returned to Port Charlotte and the gregarious Mr Rees, said unsteadily, 'I believe you knew a friend of mine. Miranda Taylor.'

He glowered. 'A friend of yours? Why the hell should I know a friend of yours?'

'She told me . . .'

'Go back where you came from, nosy bitch . . .'

The girl pulled at his arm and he tried to shake her off, but she persisted, and he turned angrily towards her. Sally heard her whisper 'drownings' and 'newspapers'. He thrust his thumbs down his belt, eyeing Sally with reluctant interest.

'And?'

'She told me that you would explain to me . . .'

He spat over her shoulder. 'You're talkin' rubbish, woman. I never laid eyes on her.' His eyes travelled her body slowly. 'You like her—one of them models?'

'No,' Sally said, trying to suppress her mounting panic. 'I'm sorry I bothered you. It was a mistake.'

She turned and walked quickly towards the gate, but he leapt from the doorway, grabbing her shoulder, his breath hot on her face.

'You came a long way for nothin',' he hissed.

'Take your hands off me!' Sally tried to wrench herself free from his hold and he paused, the secretive eyes revealing nothing, then he swore and flung her away so that she nearly fell.

'Go home, you stupid bitch,' he said and began to laugh as she fled for the gate, dragged it open and ran headlong back towards the car.

The drizzle had turned to a light rain and it blew in her face as she ran heedlessly over the slippery grass, then the cottage door slammed to, and seconds later she thought she heard the creak of the gate opening, a voice calling to her and the beat of following footsteps. Gasping for breath and half-blinded by the raindrops that lashed on her face, she plunged into the gully. The ground was growing soggier and the heels on her shoes sucked down, making her stumble and flounder.

Ahead lay her car and she flung herself at it thankfully, wrenching open the door and fumbling with the ignition. The wheels spun in the deepening quagmire, then mercifully gripped and she reversed the car and drove heedlessly over the rough ground towards the track and Sullom.

The car lurched and bucketed complainingly over the sodden turf, the track, scarcely visible when she had approached the farm, was now indistinguishable, and Sally simply drove where it looked the flattest. The wind had risen and the rain was coming down with driving force, making it difficult to see and the way more treacherous than ever. Sally strained her eyes, peering for the metal gate that she had opened on her way there, but all she could see was the rain-lashed moor and bleak skies. Sweat broke out on her forehead at the thought that even now she could be driving in circles on Mackay land. She had to get to the other side of that gate and to the pebbly track that led to the road.

There was a flash of lightning and the sky rent. Sally saw the gate some twenty yards in front of her but further over to the left. That she had long since lost the original track she was well aware and she swung the wheel, forcing the car over the treacherous, sodden ground and the many rushing rivulets of rain water that poured down from the hills. The car groaned and rocked, the wheels sinking deeper and deeper, and Sally choked back a sob.

'Just let me make it to the road,' she prayed. 'Just to the road ... please ... please.'

Her hair whipped across her eyes, blinding her as she dashed from the shelter of the car to the cumbersome gate, then her shoes slipped on the slimy turf and she fell to her knees, tearing her stockings and muddying her coat. She somehow managed to haul herself to her feet, and grasped the gate, pulling it open. The storm was at its full fury now, and the wind slammed into her, throwing her bodily back towards the car. She clambered inside it. The engine strained and surged but the car remained stationary, its wheels spinning hopelessly in the mud.

'*Please ... please ...*' she prayed. Slowly the car sucked itself clear, lumbering between the gatepost and on to what had been the silver white track winding picturesquely to the hills. Now it was a raging torrent, a collection of all the fresh streams and burns that the storm had given birth to. The car surged on for another fifty yards then, choked with mud and aflow with water, it sputtered defiantly to a halt.

With a sob, Sally grabbed hold of her shoulder-bag and stepped out into the raging catalyst of wind and rain. She was not going to stay in the car, a sitting duck for an enraged Mackay. Sullom could not be much further. Someone in that huddle of cottages would give her shelter: all she had to do was reach it.

She plunged down the slippery track, her hands and face stung by the rain and her shoes awash with the swirling brown water that poured down from the saturated hills. She tucked her head well down, her chin pressed into the collar of her coat, seeing only one step ahead of her as the storm-force wind blasted the moor, the rain blotting out all sight of Sullom, all vision of anything that wasn't twelve inches in front of her. On and on ... the struggle against the wind was almost too much. It tore at her hair, lashing it wetly across her face. In the car Sullom had only seemed ten minutes away, but on foot, battling against the storm, it seemed miles away. She felt she would never reach it. Struggling for breath she moved doggedly onward: every cell in her body felt frozen; the rain had poured down the back of her neck, sluicing into her coat and her legs and feet were numbed by the icy water.

Thunder rolled, but this time it was further away and Sally raised her head slightly. The sky was lightening and the centre of the storm was moving to the east. The wind still blasted squalls of heavy rain across the barren moor, making it difficult to see, but there, in front of her, were the crofts of Sullom. She began to run, gasping for breath and blinking the rain from her eyes, her mind empty of everything but the prospect of shelter and, if she were lucky, a telephone.

For the last few yards, the wind seemed to double in fury, whipping her coat painfully against her legs, slamming the breath from her body. She battled onwards, her vision once again limited to the path immediately in front of her feet. Then, after an endless age, she reached the first of the small crofts. It was bounded by a low stone wall and a wooden gate, and the enclosed grass was shorn and cared for. With stiff hands she pushed the gate open and waded up the path which was awash with water.

'Mercy me,' the large, motherly woman said who opened the door, staring at Sally in astonishment. 'Come in, lassie, come in. You'll catch your death, why . . . you're soaked to the skin. Come away in an' get dry.'

Numbly Sally allowed herself to be divested of her dripping coat and gratefully accepted the proffered towel to dry her face and hair.

'Lost, were you?' her benefactress asked sympathetically. 'They're cruel hills to go wanderin' in if you're not knowin' the way, an' this storm, like as not it near swept you away!'

Sally nodded, her teeth chattering so much that she couldn't reply.

'Into the kitchen with you an' have a wee dram, that'll soon set you up.'

She led Sally into a small room with plastered walls and shiny linoleum floor, and a fire of smouldering peats, and poured her a half-tumblerful of whisky.

'That's what you're needin', an' I'll make a wee cup of tea and a bite to eat.'

'You're very kind . . .' Sally said weakly.

'Ach, don't talk nonsense, lassie. Did you get caught walkin' up from the road?'

Sally shook her head, the whisky searing her throat. 'No, I came from the other direction.'

Her hostess's expression was one of open curiosity. 'From the hills?'

'I'd been to the Mackay farm and my car got bogged down . . .'

'Aye?' she said, good manners forbidding her to ask the questions she was obviously bursting with.

Sally, fortified by the whisky and slowly thawing out, said, 'It was a mistake. I thought Pete Mackay knew a friend of mine, but I was wrong.'

'Ach, yon's got no friends,' the woman said disparagingly, busily setting out scones and butter and jam on the table.

'I can understand why,' Sally said feelingly.

'Rude to you, was he?'

The kettle began to steam and she brewed the tea. 'Queer people, the Mackays. Since his wife died we hardly ever see him. The lassie comes down to the shops but she's like him, moody and bad-tempered, not a good word for nobody. Best left alone, if you ask me.'

She pushed a plate of scones and oatcakes across to Sally.

'There's plenty more where they came from, my girl.' She settled herself comfortably, her hands wrapped warmly around her mug of tea. 'Foreigner he is, came from the mainland to marry Willie Herbert's lassie. Never mixed, he didn't, used to stay up there in the hills and then she grew the same. Hardly got a word out of her, broke old Willie's heart, it did. She died last year, just before the bairn's sixteenth birthday, and since then they've gone from bad to worse. I told the minister, isn't *Christian* a young lass cooped up in them hills with only him for company. Last time he went near the place he got a mouthful of abuse for his trouble, poor man. What kind of behaviour is that? Disgustin', I call it.'

Sally, the blood throbbing painfully in her fingers and toes, wholeheartedly agreed.

'An' if he gets his thievin' hands on your car . . .' she said expressively.

'Are you on the telephone?' Sally asked, brought back to the immediate problem of how to dislodge her car before it became irretrievably bogged down.

'No, lassie, but don't worry. I'll away down to Lizzie McBain's. Her man's home today and so is her boy—they'll soon have the car movin' for you.'

'Oh, but I couldn't . . .'

'Ach, it's no trouble,' her hostess answered, well aware that she wouldn't be the one to get soaked to the skin. 'Do 'em good. You sit here by the fire an' I'll away down. Where did you say you left it?'

'Just past the iron gate.'

Sally handed her the car keys, and she was gone, impatient to share the latest news.

Sally stretched out her legs, overcome with tiredness. She knew what Jeff would call her. Stupid . . . silly . . . She grinned to herself. For once he would be right.

Chapter Ten

She awoke, stiff and aching in every limb, to the sound of the door opening and the shuffling of feet.

'Sssh now, the lassie's asleep.' Then, as Sally stirred, blinking round at them: 'Your car is outside, miss, a bitty dirty but all in one piece. I'll put the kettle on an' we can all have a wee drink an' a bite to eat.'

Behind her, a large, burly man stood uncomfortably, twisting his hat in his hands, and next to him stood a younger edition, grinning widely at her.

'An' this is Callum an' his son Kenneth. My, my, what a time of it they had! That car of yours was stuck well and truly an' old Mackay came out cursin' and swearin'.' She smiled amiably. 'I've never enjoyed myself so much for years.'

'I'm very grateful to you,' Sally said feebly, feeling the words totally inadequate to the overpowering relief she felt.

'Ach, was nothin',' Callum said shyly.

'It was a great deal, especially in this weather.' Sally looked out of the window to a picture of soft moorland lazing under a pale sun, to hills fragile behind a veil of mist, and a sky rinsed blue and clear with not a rain cloud in sight.

'We've been a wee while,' her hostess said, throwing a snowy cloth over the polished table. 'It will be a grand day tomorrow, I'm thinking.'

Her two companions agreed enthusiastically, edging round the table as fresh cakes, brown bread and jam and homemade biscuits appeared.

'I still don't know your name,' Sally said, taking cups and saucers from her hand and setting them beside the plates.

'Meg. I'm known to everyone as Meg, though I was christened Margaret Mary McAllister if the truth be known.' She paused for a minute, then said with sudden shyness: 'An' your name?'

'Sally Craig. I'm from London and staying in Port Charlotte on holiday.'

'London, is it?' Kenneth McBain said wonderingly. 'An' do you like it here?'

Sally nodded, and the elder McBain said, still standing and shifting from one foot to another. 'You stayin' at the hotel there, are you? I've heard say they've done it out ever so smart.'

'No,' Sally said, taking a large piece of cake. 'I'm staying in a cottage, the Taylors' cottage.'

He rubbed the back of his head thoughtfully. 'I don't believe I know any Taylors in Port Charlotte. New people, are they?'

'It's a holiday cottage. The people who own it are English.'

'Is that so?' he said, drawing up a chair and sitting beside Meg.

Meg poured out the tea, saying hesitantly, 'That wouldn't be any relation to the poor lassie that . . .'

'Yes,' Sally said unwillingly. 'That's why I came, really. We were friends and . . .' Her voice broke off.

'Tch,' Meg said sympathetically. 'I'm sorry that's what brought you here. Dreadful, it was. Dreadful thing to have happened.'

The two men muttered condolences and for a moment Sally felt that her outward calm would break. Then Kenneth said, 'George Cameron from Bruichladdich used to take her fishin' sometimes. He said she was a grand swimmer—an athlete, he called her.'

Meg pursed her lips. 'An' comin' from yon that's praise indeed, but Saligo . . .' She shook her head expressively. 'There's a good many drowned in Saligo. It's cruel those currents are, and they always find the bodies swept up into the Little Strand a bitty further up. I remember not so long since a young lassie from Manchester . . .'

'An' the lassie that wrote an' took all the photographs,' Kenneth said gloomily.

'But George said that Miss Taylor had been comin' here since she was seven or eight. He said she *knew* Saligo . . .'

'She did,' Sally said quietly. 'And your friend was right. She was a strong swimmer.'

'Makes no difference in Saligo,' Kenneth McBain said, fidgeting with embarrassment at speaking out so boldly. 'Local people have lost their lives there, people who have known Saligo all their lives. 'Tis a treacherous place.'

'An' you thought perhaps Pete Mackay knew your friend, did you?' Meg asked ingenuously, pouring out second cups of tea.

'Yes, but I was wrong. It couldn't have been him.'

'Ach, no,' she agreed. 'No civilized body would be havin' anythin' to do with *him*.'

'Do you know of anyone else by that name?' Sally asked hopefully.

Three heads shook in unison.

'An' who told you where he lived?' Meg asked, wanting her facts right for future gossip.

'The woman in the shop at the junction of the main road.'

Three pairs of eyes exchanged knowing looks, and Meg said spiritedly, 'Yon knew he wouldn't be who you were lookin' for. That woman is nothin' but a troublemaker! To send a young lassie up there by herself . . . and in that weather . . . Disgustin', that's what it is. Disgustin'. There was no need for it.'

'An' what will you do now?' Kenneth asked, cramming a third slice of wholemeal bread and jam into his mouth.

Sally shrugged. 'There's not much I can do. I'll probably stay on a bit longer and see more of Islay.'

'But not more of the Mackays!' Meg said merrily.

'No, thank you very much,' Sally said with feeling.

'An' him, rantin' an' ravin' an' cursin' an' swearin',' Meg crowed, her plump body beginning to rock with mirth. Then they were all laughing. Callum's tea slopping into his saucer as he gasped. '"Get off my bloody land," he said,' his eyes glistening as he began laughing again.

It was four o'clock before Sally managed to leave, and by that time she was the only one of them completely sober, and that only because she had known she had to drive back to Port Charlotte. The sound of singing interspersed with gales of laughter floated out after her, and it seemed as if the ceilidh would continue for hours, or at least until Meg's whisky ran out.

Warmed through by Meg's wee drams and overwhelmed by kindness, Sally felt buoyant as she speeded back to the cottage. As far as she was concerned, the search for Pete Mackay was over. She was becoming more and more convinced that he had only been a visitor to the island, *if* he'd ever been on the island at all, and that searching for him among the locals was a waste of time. Jeff was right: the answer to the riddle most likely lay in London and Miranda's familiar habitat, than it did in Islay. And he had promised to ring her at ten o'clock with whatever news he might have. There was nothing for her to do now but wait.

Mrs MacBride was walking down the street towards the sea, and Sally lingered by the car after she had parked, swinging her keys and waiting for her.

Sally felt there was a shade of disapproval in Mrs MacBride's eyes as she saw the muddy car parked outside the immaculately kept cottages, but her smile, when she turned to Sally, was warm and sincere.

'Had a nice day, have you?'

'Lovely,' Sally lied, not wanting to get involved with the Mackay episode again. 'Mrs MacBride, I wonder if I could ask you a question? You remember when you told me you met Miranda by the quay, immediately before you found the cottage had been broken into?'

'Aye,' Mrs MacBride said, resting her basket of groceries on the bonnet of the car.

'You said Miranda had just returned from somewhere. Where was it?'

'Ach, now you're askin'.' Her face puckered as she struggled to think. 'Kilchoman!' she said at last. 'That was it. Kilchoman.'

'Have you any idea why she should have gone over there?' Sally asked.

Mrs MacBride shrugged. 'I've not the least idea. Because she wanted to, I suppose.'

'But what is there at Kilchoman?' Sally persisted.

'Nothing, nothing at all, except a church and a graveyard, but like as not she wouldn't actually have *been* to Kilchoman, likely she would have been to the beach nearby. Yes, that would be it, the beach.' Her blue eyes cleared and she gave a sigh of satisfaction. 'Lovely beach there is, though I haven't been that way for years now, when . . .'

'What is it called?'

'Machir Bay.' A shadow fell across her face. 'Oh dear, you weren't thinkin'. . .'

'No,' Sally interrupted. 'No, I wasn't. It's all right. I just wanted to know where she had been that day.'

'Aye well, no doubt she'd been swimmin'.' Her words trailed into thin air and she picked up her basket, disconcerted.

Sally said good-bye as cheerfully as she could and, turning, let herself into the cottage. Her conversation with Mrs MacBride had re-awakened her desire to trace Miranda's last footsteps. Tomorrow morning she would drive out to Kilchoman and to Machir Bay but this evening she would stay in the cottage quietly and try to put the pieces of the puzzle together. And wait for Jeff's phone call.

She went into the kitchen, to prepare a quick meal, trying to keep her mind blank until she could think in comfort before the fire, with a tray of food on her lap. The sky was clouding over rapidly and it looked as if the few hours of sunshine were to be replaced by more rain. White-flecked ripples raced across the steely grey surface of the sea, and the small boats at the quayside plunged and reared at their moorings.

Sally laid Miranda's letter on the side of the tray, then carried her meal through into the sitting-room. As she ate, enjoying the peace and solitude and the warmth of the gas fire on her legs, she read and re-read the letter.

If I don't make it, and I mean that quite literally, Pete Mackay will explain to you what's been happening these last few weeks. I can't be any clearer or you'll be in the same position as I am.

The more she read it the more sure she was that Pete Mackay

was not someone who would be easy to find. There was more to it than that. Miranda had been deliberately obscure, but why? In case the letter fell into anyone else's hands? In case the men who ransacked An Cala should come again, and read the letter? That had to be it. It had to be something she would understand but no one else would. But in heaven's name, what?

She put the tray on the floor and curled her legs beneath her in the chair, cupping her hands around her hot drink.

We know each other so well that I don't have to put any more. I know you'll do what I want.

What would Miranda expect her to do? Sally closed her eyes, completely at a loss, then, as her mind relaxed, hovering near to sleep, she saw again the cottage as it had been with the drawers emptied and the furniture ripped, and the books . . . books tossed everywhere, the shelves swept clean . . . and the new book that Miranda must have brought to Islay with her, missing.

She opened her eyes with a start. Books. They were her passion and her chief love and Miranda knew that. The first thing she always did when visiting a house was to look at the books and that's just what Miranda would expect her to do at An Cala. Pete Mackay didn't have to be a person. She leapt from the chair and, starting with the bookshelves in the alcove near the window, began to search with trembling hands through the titles and authors. There was a book by Esther McCracken and one by Stephen McFarlane but nothing by a Pete Mackay. She opened a glass-paned bookcase with its neat rows of leather-bound classics, reading through the titles slowly, but there was nothing. Nothing at all. She rocked back on her heels, considering.

Perhaps it was a character, not a title or an author, but if it was, it must be one that Miranda would expect Sally to know.

Slowly she went back to the chair, gazing at the books before her and struggling to remember a Pete Mackay. The task of flicking through each book would be phenomenal—there were easily three or four hundred in the cottage. Outside, the light was paling and the hills on the far side of the bay were growing darker. She turned on a lamp and pulled her chair closer to the fire. Pete Mackay . . .

It rang no sort of bell in her mind at all. She continued to sit, staring at the orange glow of the flames, struggling to think of any book that she had read which had contained that name.

The phone ringing loudly in the quiet cottage made her jump, and she ran across to it, tense with anticipation, longing to hear Jeff's voice.

'I have a call for you, will you hold?' The operator's voice was thin and high, the line crackling so badly that she could hardly hear.

'Yes, yes . . . Oh Jeff, how super to hear you!'

'More than I can say for you. You sound as if you're in Siberia not the Hebrides.'

'I know. Isn't it dreadful! You'll have to yell.'

'I *am* yelling!'

'When are you coming back?'

'I can't hear you, Sal. What did you say?'

'When are you coming back?' she shouted down the phone.

'Saturday.'

'*Saturday.*' she echoed incredulously. 'But that's *days* away . . .'

The line was riddled with interference and then she heard Jeff say, 'So I might as well hang on till he gets back. This friend of his in the flat says Carpenter definitely went with a Pete Mackay . . .'

'I don't understand. Went where?'

'Paris apparently. His friend says they're coming back Friday so I'll hang on . . .'

'What about the briefcase?'

'I can't hear you, Sal. What did you say?'

'The *briefcase.*'

'Tell you when I see you, but don't worry any more. Understand?'

She gripped the phone tighter, pressing it against her ear until it hurt.

'*Tell me now.* I can't wait till Saturday not knowing.'

'It will keep. Sally . . .'

'Jeff, you're hiding something from me. What is it?'

There was a slight pause and then he said, 'Nothing, only that

Miranda and Gregory were more than good friends, and something else. Gregory was epileptic . . .'

'What the hell has that to do with it?' she yelled, frustrated by the bad line, by the distance between them, by everything.

'Just that the drowning could have been an accident after all, if Gregory had an attack and Miranda tried to save him . . . he'd be far to heavy for her in those waters . . .'

'But the cottage, Jeff. And the letter?'

'Look, Sally, talking like this is impossible. I can hardly hear you. I'm coming back to Islay on Saturday and we'll spend a week together. There's nothing more to worry about. Believe me, Sally, I'm not having you on. We've built a mountain out of a mole-hill. All Pete Mackay will be able to tell you is that Miranda *was* having an affair with Gregory. Don't brood on it—and remember that I love you.'

'Remember what?' she shouted as his voice faded.

'*I love you*, and I'll see you on Saturday. Take care of yourself.'

The line went dead and she lowered the receiver slowly, the sense of anti-climax overwhelming her. Jeff was no fool. If he said they'd built a mountain out of a molehill the chances were that he was right. And Miranda in love with Gregory Phillips? Impossible though it seemed, wasn't it better than her being in love with Jeff?

She went to her chair and sat down, wondering once more why Miranda had been so adamant that Jeff should not be told where she had gone to. Especially if she loved Gregory. Did she fear Jeff would follow and upset her arrangements? Would Jeff have been too jealous about it? The more she puzzled, the more perturbed she became. If only she could get rid of these doubts about Jeff . . . if only. She sighed heavily, there was nothing more she could do until Jeff returned and could tell her what Pete Mackay had said. But the doubts remained to torment her.

Chapter Eleven

The next morning dawned bright and clear, the sun glinting on the smooth surface of the sea and the far-away hills basking in golden light. There was no trace of the storm and the rain of the previous day. Sally lifted the curtains away from the window so that she could enjoy the view. Down at the quayside nets were being brought in and she could hear the shouts of the children on the half-moon of shingle hectoring the fishermen.

The pleasant feeling aroused by the sun and sparkling clear air faded as she remembered Jeff's phone call. She went back to bed and hugged her arms around her knees. No matter how hard she tried, she couldn't accept Jeff's advice to stop worrying: she wouldn't be able to do that until she saw him again. Meanwhile she would continue as she had originally planned. Today she would visit Kilchoman and tomorrow . . . tomorrow she would go on her own to Saligo Bay.

She dressed hurriedly, for despite the sun there was still a chill in the morning air, and began to make herself a breakfast of bacon, eggs and tomatoes.

'Would you like a nice fish?' Mrs MacBride asked, standing at the doorway with a wet parcel in her hand.

'Yes, please,' Sally answered, wondering how to gut a freshly caught fish.

Mrs MacBride walked through into the kitchen, depositing her package on the formica work-top. 'I wondered if you'd heard the news?'

'What news?' Sally stopped turning the bacon to stare at her.

'About Pete Mackay.'

The kitchen spun dizzily around her but she managed to keep standing upright and said carefully, 'No I haven't. What's happened to him?'

'Taken to hospital this morning. Quite bad, Angus was sayin'.'

'To *hospital?*' Sally asked, unbelievingly.

'Aye, that's right. I just heard now.'

'But what with? He was quite healthy when I saw him yesterday.'

'Is that so?' Mrs MacBride said, her blue eyes alight with interest. 'Well, he's in the hospital now and no mistake.'

'But what *with?*'

She shrugged. 'Old age, I expect.'

Sally stared at her, wondering if she was hearing right. 'But he couldn't be more than forty or forty-five!'

'Tch, nonsense! He was ninety if he was a day!'

Sally lifted the frying pan from the hot plate and said with forced control, 'Mrs MacBride, *which* Pete Mackay are you talking about?'

'Why, old Pete Mackay away over at Kiells.'

Sally's heartbeats gradually returned to normal and she began to dish up her bacon and eggs on to a warmed plate. 'I'm sorry, we were at cross purposes. I thought you meant somebody else.'

'An' did you find another one?' Mrs MacBride asked, following Sally across to the table.

'Oh yes, I found another one all right, but he didn't know Miranda.'

'Aye?' Mrs MacBride waited expectantly, but Sally simply said: 'I think the Pete Mackay Miranda mentioned was a London friend, Mrs MacBride. I'm not looking for him any more.'

'That's a sensible lassie,' she soothed. 'No good can come of it. What's happened has happened and nothing in the world can alter it, more's the pity.'

There was no reply to that, and Sally began eating her breakfast with Mrs MacBride sitting by her side.

'An' will you be takin' all her things back with you?' she asked after a little while.

'I haven't really thought about it, but I suppose so. There isn't so much to take.'

Mrs MacBride sniffed and said with a catch in her voice, 'I'd appreciate it if you would—each time I go in her room and see them there it gives me a start, an' then I get to thinkin'. . .'

'I'll take them back with me,' Sally said, wishing that Mrs MacBride would leave her with her own thoughts.

'An' her books and postcards and everythin'?'

'Postcards?' Sally asked sharply, wondering for a minute if she had overlooked something.

'Aye, those cards she bought. Of the church and graveyards . . .' Her voice trailed away, and then she said in little more than a whisper, 'Strange she should buy those just before . . .'

'Mrs MacBride,' Sally said firmly, 'it was nothing more than a coincidence. I dare say the bulk of the postcards available in Islay are pictures of old churches and Celtic crosses.'

Mrs MacBride pursed her lips, feeling rebuffed and Sally said hastily, 'But you're right about moving them all away. I'll pack everything this evening.'

Suitably appeased, Mrs MacBride rose to her feet. 'Well, I hope you have a fine day. I'm away to Bowmore to see a mannie about my roof. It's been leakin' terrible an' I must get it fixed before the winter comes. It takes so long for them to come an' do things nowadays.' She smiled. 'An' don't forget your fish, it will make a nice tea for you.'

'No, I won't,' Sally promised.

Mrs MacBride let herself out, leaving Sally alone with her thoughts. She had forgotten all about the blank postcards in the drawer upstairs, and after putting her plate into the sink she went up to have another look at them.

One was of Port Ellen from Kilnaughton Bay, and showed a deserted sandy cove, blue sea and some indistiguishable buildings on the far side of the bay. The sand was coloured an improbable yellow and Sally could only imagine that Miranda had bought it in a hurry. Another one was of the cross and church at Kildalton and the third was of a graveyard of neat, uniform headstones. She turned the card over to read the small print at the back. It was a

Naval cemetery at Kilchoman, the graves belonging to the dead of two ships torpedoed off Islay in the First World War.

Thoughtfully she put them back in the drawer, together with the gloves and the few pieces of jewellery that Miranda had brought with her and that the men who had broken into An Cala had left completely untouched. She picked up a heavy gold bracelet, weighing it in her hand. This drawer, like the others, had been emptied, but the bracelet had been found on the floor, as had the string of pearls and the tie pin with the sapphire stone that Miranda had worn on her suit. It hardly seemed credible that anyone who had broken in should regard them so lightly: it was obvious that they were the genuine article and not costume jewellery.

Jeff hadn't come up with a theory to explain away the ransacking of the cottage when he had told her that they had made a mountain out of a mole-hill and that there was nothing to worry about. Wondering what his explanation would be, she closed the drawer sharply. A car ride would be good for her, the pure sea air of Kilchoman would clear her mind. She picked up her cardigan and shoulder-bag, closed the cottage door and made for her car.

The drive certainly swept the cobwebs away. The road had crossed the moors, passing a large loch, its banks deep in rushes with not even a bird to dispel the eerie loneliness, then it had petered out behind the high, grass-covered dunes and the roaring Atlantic. Sally parked the car when she could go no further, wondering whether to walk over the dunes to the beach or up the narrow path that swung away from the sea and towards Kilchoman church. After a moment's hesitation she started up the rough track.

The path was little used and the grass grew high between the sandy pebbles, the feathery wild flowers that massed the steep banks brushing her legs as she strolled leisurely onwards.

To the left of her, inland, the land rolled in lush green hills, merging in the distance into the purple of the heather and the gleam of a lonely loch.

On her right the ground rose steeply into the towering cliffs that barred the sea from sight. There was nobody about and the only buildings she could see were a large whitewashed farm flying a

Union Jack and the dark stone church a mile or so ahead. As the farm drew nearer she passed a field of cows, their coats glossy beneath the warm rays of the sun that were making her hot and uncomfortable in her heavy cardigan. They gave her an idle glance, flicking their tails, and continuing to graze peacefully, a flock of birds on the farmyard fence keeping them company.

A large notice explained the apparent eccentricity of the Union Jack. The building was not a farm as she had supposed, but a Coastguard station and a fierce labrador ran the length of its chain, barking angrily at her as she passed the gate. She quickened her steps, the path winding lazily down into a shallow combe with more well-fed cattle in the fields, and seawards a wild expanse of grass and thistles and the snowy white, bobbing heads of the cotton plants.

The path descended lower, twisting between high banks of wild flowers. She could smell step-mother blossom and hedge parsley and the faint whiff of flax. The church faded from view and there was only the grass and the flowers, the dusty track in front of her and the scudding clouds, high in the brilliant sky.

Gradually she climbed again, the path winding between overgrown banks of dandelions and rushes, the water glittering over smooth pebbles, the sound pleasant and cool in the still air. The breeze blew stronger as she neared the crown of the hill and she could taste the tang of salt on her lips.

A little way ahead was the church in its walled enclosure, and two adjoining crofts. Behind them soared an overhang of rock, gloomy and forbidding even in the strong sunlight, softened here and there by heather, and gashed by gleaming runnels of water where streams ran down to the sea. As she drew nearer she saw that the land seawards was fenced off and a small notice said: 'Naval Cemetery. Please Close the Gate.' A grassy footpath crossed fields of cows towards the lip of the cliffs, and silhouetted against the blue sky was the stark white of a granite cross.

She paused, then turned to the church, climbing the still rising ground till she reached the surrounding wall. The backdrop of cliff was more oppressive than ever, and now that she was closer she could see clefts choked with heather and moss and crags sheering steeply.

The churchyard was heavily overgrown, the graves set closely together, the dates on most of them at least a hundred years old. Picking her way through and over them, she crossed to the far side of the church where the ground shelved suddenly and a blank stone cross predominated. It had the same circle ringing the centre of the cross and the same sort of carving on it that the Kildalton Cross had had in the photograph Mr Rees had shown her, but whereas the other had been cleaned so that the intricate patterns and figures showed clearly, this one was covered with lichen, the carving blurred and indecipherable. To Sally, its overgrown appearance only added to its beauty and she spent fifteen or twenty minutes plucking the moss carefully away, exposing more of the pattern below. It was an occupation she could have continued all morning if she had had no other purpose in mind, but this would hardly have been Miranda's reason for visiting Kilchoman. Reluctantly she gave the cross a final brush with her hand and turned towards the doorway of the church.

As she stepped from the sunlight into the cool shadows, she knew at once that the church would have held nothing of interest for Miranda.

The walls were plain, the decorative arches simple, the pews gleaming wood, the air redolent of wax and polish. There was nothing here that would have induced Miranda to make the rough walk. Mrs MacBride had been right when she had said that the beach would have been Miranda's only reason for going to Kilchoman. Whenever she and Miranda had gone away together they had spent the days differently. Sally in the local churches and historic ruins, Miranda lazily soaking up the sun on the beach.

Sally let the door swing to behind her, grateful for the warm sun on her face as she shut her eyes and kept them shut, suppressing the sobs that rose in her throat as her grief swept over afresh.

Heavy-hearted she set off back towards the car, closing the churchyard gate behind her, ignoring the footpath to the cemetery.

She had had too much of death for the time being; what she needed now was the healing balm of sun and sea and fresh air.

The moors stretched out purple and green in the distance, gradually merging into a blue haze beneath the heat of midday, and ahead of her, down the sandy path, the only shadows were of the waving fronds of leaves and the dancing heads of yellow and blue flowers. There was no other protection from the sun's rays and she slipped off her cardigan, wishing that she had brought her bikini with her so that she could cool off after her walk.

By the time she had clambered over the dunes and down to the beach she was hot and tired, but the effort was well worth it. The curve of the silent bay lay open to the Atlantic surf, the breakers rolling in over unsullied silver sand, the cliffs forming perfect, sheltered havens for sunbathing. She slipped off her sandals, running down to the foaming waves. High above her a fulmar glided on an up-draught of air, and she knew that she had found Miranda's reason for visiting Kilchoman. It had nothing to do with the church or cemetery on the postcards; she had come simply for the beach and the sea, and the joy of bathing undisturbed.

She stood still, the waves creaming in flecked ripples around her legs, the dull roar of the sea filling her ears and heart till she felt they would burst, the feeling of peace and relaxation gone as quickly as it had come. She found she was trembling; a little way further up the coast lay Saligo Bay, and agonizing images crowded her mind, chilling her flesh; her heart thudding painfully, she rushed from the surf, running over the sand, her only desire to shut out the sound and the smell and the sight of the hungry sea. Hastily she slipped her feet into her sandals, climbing over the spiky sea grass of the dunes and back to the car. She should never have come, her loss was too fresh, too bitter . . .

The pain within her softened gradually, to be replaced by numbness as she drove across the moors back to Port Charlotte. Jeff was right. She was silly and stupid. To try and follow Miranda's footsteps could do nothing but intensify grief. Miranda was dead and dwelling on the fact would only sink her into morbid depression. She bit her lip, speeding past the loch with unseeing eyes. She would ring Jeff, tell him she was leaving the island and for him to stay in London and wait for her there. She needed the reassurance that their love would continue away from Islay and Miranda's memory. To have made a decision brought her a certain amount of calm, and soon she saw Port Charlotte in the distance, blissfully unaware of the large car that loomed behind her in the distance, never drawing nearer and never letting her out of sight.

Chapter Twelve

It was only two o'clock by the time she reached Port Charlotte. She parked outside the hotel and went inside to use the telephone, but there was no reply from the number Jeff had given her to ring. Disappointed, she made her way back towards the reception desk, to be met by Mr Rees, stout-booted, a pile of books in his arms.

'Why, Miss Craig, what a lovely surprise! Just been in for lunch, have you?'

'No, I've been using the telephone.'

'Aah, absence making the heart grow fonder, is it?' He beamed good-naturedly. 'Where did you get to this morning—anywhere interesting?'

'I drove over to Kilchoman and had a look at the church. There's a cross there similar to the one at Kildalton.'

'*And* a Standing Stone a little way outside the churchyard. Was over there myself last week. Interesting, very interesting.' He set his books down on the hall carpet. 'Had a frustrating morning myself, been trying to get over to Boonahahvin and the damned road's private.'

'Boonahahvin?' Sally asked vaguely.

He rifled through his books, selecting a battered, leather-bound volume bristling with bookmarks.

'Apparently it used to be the only sea port on the east coast of the island.' Balancing the open book precariously he reached for his back pocket and his ordnance survey map of Islay. Sally took the book from him while he spread the map on the wall, pointing to a spot a few miles above Port Askaig where no roads or paths were indicated.

'Foot of the river the name means, and here'—his finger traced the thin blue line of a river into the hills—'here is where there was a market town. Nothing there now, of course, only the name. Margadale. But *here*'—his finger stopped at the tiny place name of Gortonoid—'here is still the path that led over to Margadale and Boonahahvin.' He folded the map, put it beneath his arm, and reached for the book. 'See here, page thirty-nine, it says there are still traces of the ancient public road that led from Killinallen and Gortonoid to Margadale where the great Market Fairs were held. Packmen came from great distances to sell here, some even from London. Well, you can see that if you go to Loch Gruinart. You can follow the footpath from Killinallen to Gortonoid, and with a compass you could walk the rest of the way through the hills to Boonahahvin and back down to Port Askaig.' He paused for breath. 'Looking forward to it I was . . .'

'What happened?' Sally asked, studying the map and nearly as interested as Mr Rees himself.

'*Private*,' he said with disgust. 'Got as far as Killinallen, only to be turned back.'

Sally frowned, reading the passage in the book again. 'But it says here that the road is an ancient public road, I would have thought you would still have been given access.'

'Might have stood a chance if it had been a farmer but it was a woman and she was quite adamant. Private, utterly private,' he said, mimicking the way she had spoken. His shoulders dropped. 'So there you are, no tramp across to Boonahahvin.'

'I'm sure you'll find something else to do that you'll enjoy just as much,' Sally said sympathetically.

His face brightened. 'There's Dunyvaig. I could take you to Dunyvaig.'

'What about Mrs Rees?' Sally asked dubiously.

'Not to worry, not to worry,' he said breezily. 'Angela has a headache and is lying down. She'll be glad to get me out of the way.'

Sally smiled. 'All right then, Mr Rees. You show me Dunyvaig.'

There were a few clouds in the sky now and it was slightly

cooler as they walked across to Mr Rees's car. The light breeze ruffled the azure surface of the sea and stirred the masses of begonias that grew in earthenware tubs at either side of the hotel's doorway. The faint scent of the flowers drifted after them, mingling with the tang of the sea and the faint whiff of a nearby peat stack.

Mr Rees opened the door for her, sliding back the roof of his car, before turning on the ignition and rolling slowly out into the narrow road.

'I'm glad I came here, very glad. Angela wanted to go to Benidorm but it wouldn't have been my cup of tea. Promised her she can go next spring. This is what I like. Rooting out a bit of history, a bit of romance. Not enough of it in the world.'

Sally laughed and he blushed. 'Not the romance of, er . . .' He coughed. 'Not *that* sort of romance, but the romance of strange places and old tales . . .'

'I know exactly what you mean, Mr Rees.'

'Wish my wife did,' he said. 'Take Dunyvaig for instance, steeped in romance it is. The Lordship of the Isles was a maritime power and Dunyvaig was built on the promontory at the entrance to Lagavulin Bay where the ships were harboured. It must have seen its share of battles and sieges and victories.'

'This Lordship of the Isles, Mr Rees, what was it? I've kept hearing the name Somerled but I don't know the full story.'

'Well, briefly, and I mean briefly because to tell you the story as it should be told would take till midnight. Somerled is the father of the Clan Donald of Islay. He was a warrior prince of the twelfth century and his father was King of Argyll. At this time the Norse had invaded the Western Isles and it was Somerled who finally drove them out.'

'That must have taken some doing. The Norsemen were great fighters, weren't they?'

'Tremendous, tremendous, but Somerled had brains as well as brawn. The strength of the Vikings was in their sea power, their ships; the Celts' boats were frail little things at that time. Somerled set to building a fleet of real fighting ships, smaller than the Vikings but strong and powerful, and on the night of Epiphany 1156 he sailed up the west coast of Islay and routed the Vikings once and for all.'

'That explains the emblem that I see everywhere, of the little boat with four men in.'

'That's it, Somerled and his sons—they use it on everything. Well, Somerled berthed his fleet at Lagavulin and from then on his quarrel was with David, the King of Scotland. He was influenced by the Norman King of England, Henry the First, and this didn't suit the Celts. When David died and was succeeded by Malcolm, a boy of thirteen, Somerled and his men sailed up the Firth of Clyde and marched to Paisley to speak to him.'

'And . . .?'

'Murdered,' said Mr Rees, as if the dreadful deed had taken place that very day. 'Somerled was murdered during the night in his tent. His son ruled after him to be succeeded by *his* son, Donald the First of Islay, and he in turn by his son, Angus the Great.'

'I really don't know how you remember it all,' Sally said admiringly as they drove away from the sea and down the straight road across the moor to Port Ellen.

'Nothing better to do with my time, I suppose,' he said sheepishly. 'Anyway, Dunyvaig was built by Donald the First and remained a key stronghold up to the seventeenth century. The last chief of Clan, Donald of Islay, was Sir James of Dunyvaig. His younger brother defended it against attack from the Earl of Argyll, but cannon was used to breach it and it couldn't hold out. After that it gradually deteriorated until all that's left is what you see today. But something of the spirit lives on, at least I like to think so. Unfortunately Angela doesn't see it in the same light . . .'

The stiff breeze fanned Sally's cheeks, lifting her hair, and Mr Rees said considerately, 'Would you like me to put up the hood?'

She shook her head. 'No thanks. This is super, honestly.'

The moors were utterly still, the only movement being the occasional flight of a bird and the huge clusters of flowers that crowded the banks of the road, bobbing beneath the heat of the sun. They sailed into the untidy streets of Port Ellen, Mr Rees seeming to have little or no regard for the local speed limit, and out on to the glorious coast road where an aquamarine sea splashed lazily against craggy creeks and islets and silver-white rocks strewn with gleaming seaweed.

'There it is,' Mr Rees said, with a sigh of pure pleasure.

The headland was bathed in sunlight, the grass a rich green against the grey of the cliffs, the ruins of Dunyvaig standing magnificently above the sea that foamed at the rocks far below.

'I've heard it said that when two men of Clan Donald meet within those shattered walls, they still drink a solemn toast to the Noble House of Islay.'

Sally smiled. 'I was under the impression that it was a custom you'd begun to follow yourself.'

His ruddy cheeks deepened. 'Now, now, Miss Craig, you mustn't believe all you hear. Though I must admit that, when Angela and I came the first time, it was a bitterly cold day and a little refreshment was needed.'

He parked the car beneath the crimson berries of a hawthorn tree, and they walked over the springy turf, thick with harebells and golden broom, up on to the headland, where the sea breeze ruffled the long grasses that grew among the broken walls of Dunyvaig.

'What brought you here, Miss Craig?' he asked, helping her up a steep incline.

She paused for breath. The coastline from the Mull of Oa to Kildalton stretched out before her, the sea shading through bars of sunlight from palest green to deepest emerald. The raw hurt of the morning had mercifully numbed.

'A girl friend of mine was drowned here a few weeks ago.'

His kind face, filled with embarrassed concern. 'Oh dear, I'm sorry, very sorry. I wasn't meaning to be rude. Terrible thing to have happened. Terrible.'

Sally leant against the cool stone of a crumbling tower, her fingers pulling idly at the moss. 'What made it more dreadful was that I didn't believe it to have been an accident. That's why I came.'

He sat down clumsily, his usually beaming face solemn and drawn.

'I don't know what to say to you, Miss Craig, I really don't. If I'd known you had all this trouble . . .'

'Please don't worry. You've done me a favour bringing me out like this. Besides, I think I was wrong. Jeff rang me last night from London and said we'd jumped to conclusions. So I shall go home and try to forget it all.'

'I see,' he said, his eyes still full of genuine concern. 'Still, if there's anything I can do, to help, anything at all . . .'

'You could tell me *why* the Earl of Argyll besieged the castle.'

His face brightened. 'Avarice, Miss Craig, man's avarice. Islay was a rich plum and the Earl of Argyll, together with his friend, Sir John of Calder, wanted to add it to their own vast lands. At this time Sir James of Dunyvaig was safely in prison and only the younger brother was left to hold the fort. He moved into Dunyvaig with his family and handful of clansmen, determined to hold out to the bitter end. Calder arrived, made an immediate assault on the castle with cannons and ammunition and, as I said before, breached the walls. He then celebrated by rounding up a few of the locals and beheading them. Probably over there.' He pointed to a smooth and level piece of turf.

'And that was the end of the House of Islay?'

'Nearly. Sir James did escape from prison and return to Islay but not for long. Argyll had the support of the King and Sir James was driven into exile. The local people can still show you the point where Sir James and nine of his men sailed from Islay for the last time, fleeing under cover of darkness for the safety of Ireland.'

There was silence, broken only by the waves beating on the rocks far below. Sally picked up a smooth stone, tossing it far out above the sea, watching it as it spun downwards, sinking immediately. Mr Rees joined her and she reached for another, skimming it high above the creaming surf, watching it splash and sink without trace.

The sun was beginning to move slowly westwards and Sally said, 'I think we should be getting back now. Mrs Rees will probably have recovered from her headache and be wondering where you are.'

'True, true.' He stood up, dusting his hands on his trousers. 'We'll leave Dunyvaig to the sea and the winds and return to civilization. Perhaps you'd have dinner with us tonight at the hotel?'

Sally shook her head. 'No, I don't think so, thank you. I've a lot of packing to do and I want to catch the early ferry in the morning.'

'You're going so soon?' Mr Rees asked with raised eyebrows.

'Yes. I think I've been rather stupid in coming. There was nothing for me to find.'

'Not quite with you,' Mr Rees said, helping her down the steep bank towards the road.

'My friend wrote to me shortly before her . . . accident. She said if anything happened to her, Pete Mackay would explain. It made me think something was wrong and so I came here looking for this Pete Mackay.'

'And?'

'Apparently he's a London friend. Jeff rang me last night, saying he'd found him and that there was nothing to worry about. He said I'd been making mountains out of mole-hills.'

'Probably quite right too,' Mr Rees agreed good-naturedly. 'But in the circumstances . . . well, it was natural of you to come . . . I understand how you must have felt. Might be able to see you off in the morning, Angela and I are going over to Jura for the day . . . do you know that it was on Jura that H G Wells wrote his novel *1984?* He bought a house there . . .'

Like a flood tide, Mr Rees's words washed over her as they drove towards the misty purple of the moors.

He asked her again if she would join them for dinner but Sally was adamant and he dropped her at the village shop, promising to keep a look out for her in the morning.

Having bought some fresh bread, and a huge chunk of the island cheese Sally hurried down the cobbled street, anxious to phone Jeff again and tell him she planned to leave the island.

He didn't sound as pleased as she had expected. 'But I'll be back by Saturday. We could have the whole of next week together.'

'We can still have next week together, Jeff. But not here. Everywhere I go there is the sea and . . .'

'Okay, if that's how you feel, Sally, I understand. But you'll have to collect my case from the hotel. What time do you expect to be in London?'

'I don't know, I may stay overnight somewhere . . .'

'Ring me as soon as you arrive in London and I'll meet you. This Pete Mackay is a friend of Carpenter's, they're in Paris till Saturday and so we should be able to see him together . . . Sally? Are you there? Sally . . .'

'I'm here,' she said dully.

'Well, cheer up, for goodness sake. Does the prospect of seeing me again plunge you into such despair?'

She laughed. 'Of course not. It's just Gregory and Miranda . . .'

'Stop worrying. It will all be sorted out by the weekend and I love you and we'll go somewhere super next week, where there are mountains and rivers and . . .'

'No sea.'

'No sea,' he agreed gently.

'I'll have to go now, Jeff. I've my things to pack and Miranda's, and your suitcase to collect . . .'

'All right, darling. Good night.'

'Good night,' she said, cradling the receiver in her hand long after the line had gone dead.

She packed the cases and stowed them away in the boot of the car and then went in search of Mrs MacBride.

'Going?' Mrs MacBride said with raised eyebrows.

'Yes, in the morning. I've packed all Miranda's things so they won't bother you any more, and I'll leave a note out for the milkman. I've been paying him daily so there's no money owing.'

'Well, no doubt you're doin' the best thing,' Mrs MacBride said, untying her apron. 'The mannie from Bowmore has just been about my roof. Says he can't possibly do it before November. As for the lavatory, he didn't even look at it, just said it's not worth doing at all!'

'Lavatory?' Sally asked vaguely.

'Aye, so maybe you'll tell Mrs Taylor what he said.'

'I'm sorry, I've not understood you. Why should I tell Mrs Taylor?'

'Why, because it's her lavatory of course!' Mrs MacBride said, busily folding up her apron. 'Though why she should have wanted it seeing to in the first place beats me. She'd have done better to use it for a tool shed.'

Faint light glimmered into Sally's understanding. 'Oh, I see. You mean there's an outside loo at An Cala?'

Mrs MacBride nodded. 'Have you never been outside the back door?'

Sally shook her head.

'Lot's of people still use 'em, though I did hear old Jack MacGregor keeps hens in his since he had his bathroom put in. They're immediately adjoining the kitchen wall. You just take one step out of the back door and then another step to the right for the lavatory door. Ever so convenient, nearly like having one inside the house. Can't understand all the fuss to have bathrooms put in, spending money for the sake of it, I think it is. Anyway, when you go, just drop the key in the letterbox and have a word with Mrs Taylor; it will save me writin' to her.'

'Yes, I will. Good night, Mrs MacBride.'

''Bye, lassie, an' take care.'

Sally went back to the car, driving it up to the hotel to collect Jeff's suitcase. There was no sign of Mr and Mrs Rees and she left the book he had lent Jeff with the receptionist. By the time she had heaved Jeff's suitcase on to the back seat of the car the sun was setting and the village looked sad and melancholy. Sally shivered, driving as quickly as she could over the rough cobbles towards the welcoming gleam of light in An Cala's windows. The night wind from the sea held the first damp pinpricks of rain and she fumbled hurriedly with her key, anxious for a warm drink and the comfort of the fire. As she made herself a milky cocoa in the small kitchen, gusts of wind blew against the window, rattling the glass, with drops of rain sliding slowly downwards.

She sat, sipping the hot drink, thinking. Then she put her mug down, wrapped her cardigan closely about her and opened the back door, stepping out into the darkness.

Immediately to the right of her was the bare wood of the lavatory door. She lifted the latch and pushed it open. At least she would be able to tell Jeff that she had searched everywhere, however improbable the place seemed. The glow from the kitchen window enabled her to see a switch and she pressed it down, flooding the lavatory with bright light. The walls and ceiling were freshly whitewashed and the floor was swept clean, testifying to the thoroughness with which Mrs MacBride carried out her duties. The lavatory itself did not look so very old; it had a low cistern and Sally imagined that Mrs Taylor must have had it newly installed when she bought the cottage. She doubted very much that it was impossible to repair as Mrs MacBride had said, and pushed the handle down out of curiosity. There was a thud and a grating noise but nothing else.

With one hand she lifted the corner of the cistern and peered inside. The smell of stagnant water rose unpleasantly in the air and a piece of string appeared to be tying the inside workings together. She was just about to slide the lid back again when she saw beneath the flickering water a dark object attached to the string. Very tentatively she pulled. As she did so a bulky polythene package sucked itself free of the shallow water, and very gingerly Sally took hold of it, her hands shaking as she carried it outside into the cold air. Whatever it was, it was well wrapped and it was solid.

She stumbled back into the kitchen, her heart beating painfully in her throat. Slamming the door behind her, she put her find gently on to the table. With trembling hands she undid the tightly wrapped polythene. Beneath it was a second layer, and she undid it carefully, the heavy object taking shape in her hands. Even before she lifted it from its last protective covering she knew what it was.

Gleaming unrealistically beneath the bright electric light, perfectly dry and perfectly usable, was a pistol. Gingerly she put it down on the table, staring at it uncomprehendingly.

It was a small pistol, handbag size, the kind a woman would

use, and in a little leather bag were bullets. With legs that only half supported her she went to the telephone and asked for Jeff's number.

The phone rang and rang and then the operator's voice, high pitched and impersonal, said, 'I'm getting no reply from that number.'

'Please ... try another few minutes ...'

She willed Jeff to answer the phone but it was no use.

'I'm sorry there is still no reply.'

Numbly she placed the receiver back on the rest and went into the kitchen. It hadn't gone away: it still lay there, black and solid and deadly. She turned, not wanting to look at it a minute longer. If she had been so frightened for her life that she had had to resort to possessing a pistol for self-protection, then she would have done what Miranda had done. Hide the hideous thing out of sight until it was needed, and out of sight of anyone who would break in.

One thing was for sure. She wouldn't be going home now. Instead, she picked up the gun, and pushed it to the back of a drawer in the dresser.

Chapter Thirteen

This was the explanation for Miranda's peculiar behaviour in the weeks before she had come to Islay. She had been frightened, so frightened that she had sought refuge here, giving Sally strict instructions to tell no one of her whereabouts. Yet Gregory Phillips had found her—had it been Gregory she had been afraid of? Sally's head throbbed with the effort of thinking. It couldn't have been Gregory. They had discussed him on the way to the station the day Miranda had left London, and there had been no inference to suggest that she was terrified of him. And there was the ransacking of An Cala, Sally's hands began to sweat: *that* was why Miranda had the gun. She had had something in her possession, something someone else wanted, at any price . . .

She closed her eyes, her brain a kaleidoscope of half-formed possibilities. Again the doubt came to torment her. Miranda couldn't have been terrified of Jeff, could she? *Could she?* No . . . No . . . the thought could not be borne.

What could Miranda possibly have brought with her that would cost her her life? There was no answer and Sally tried once more to telephone Jeff but without success. She fetched a blanket down from the bedroom, turned off the light, and settled herself as comfortably as possible in the armchair, determined not to go to bed until she had spoken to him.

The light from the flickering fire cast a rosy glow on the walls, and the heat made her drowsy. Despite herself, she dozed off into a light sleep, waking with a start as heavy footsteps and loud voices passed the window. They faded rapidly away and Sally peered at her watch. Stiffly she pushed the blanket away and reached for the telephone. The number rang and rang but no one answered. With a feeling she didn't want to acknowledge, she buried herself once more beneath the rough warmth of the blanket. There was no reason for her to feel slighted because he had gone out somewhere, or to be so hurt and so miserable . . . There was no reason for the finger of suspicion . . .

Sally closed her eyes again, willing him to return to the flat. She would wait till 12.30 am and try again. If he wasn't there by then she was going to bed. Her body ached with tiredness. There had been the long walk to Kilchoman in the morning and then all the scrambling about at Dunyvaig in the afternoon. All she wanted to do was sleep; perhaps in the morning everything would seem simpler, clearer. She curled her legs beneath her, pulling the blankets up under her chin. Half an hour later she knew it was useless. Despite the desperate tiredness of her body, her mind would not rest. Once more she reached for the telephone, disturbing a sleepy operator, and once more the phone rang and rang unanswered. Wearily she replaced the receiver, refusing to speculate on why he was not sleeping at home. He would explain to her when he saw her. So much had happened so soon . . .

Biting her lip, she walked into the kitchen to make herself a hot drink, studiously avoiding the drawer with its ghastly contents. If only she could have shared her discovery with Jeff she would have been able to sleep. As it was . . . she walked to the window. Any action to dispel her gloomy thoughts.

The light from the full moon streamed softly across the rooftops of the nearby cottages. The dark shape of a cat jumped from a garden wall, darting across the rough grass and out of sight. Somewhere an owl hooted, the sound lonely and melancholy in the still night air.

She shivered, her eyes drawn unwillingly to the drawer. Deliberately she turned off the light and walked back into the darkened living-room. She stood at the window there, gazing out across the great space of the bay, the moonlight gleaming on the pale foam that was the dividing line between sea and shore.

Where was Jeff? Why hadn't he phoned? Why? Why? Why?

Abruptly she reached for her coat. A walk might help.

The waves surged softly, the only sound apart from that of the owl which still called somewhere to the left of her. She walked down towards the half-moon of shingle at the jetty's edge. Here the water lapped gently on to the smooth pebbles on the shore-line. Behind her the village was an obscure mass of black shapes with only two pinpricks of light to show she wasn't the only one awake and restless.

She glanced at her watch. It was 1.25 am. Surely he would be home by now? And if he wasn't . . .

Deliberately she shut the thought from her mind, walking out on to the jetty, the water slapping softly at the stone walls, the light spray dampening her cheeks and stinging her lips with the taste of salt. All was still. She stood, shoulders hunched, gazing unseeingly at the luminous black mass of heaving waves, depression replacing the fear and excitement she had felt earlier.

A long time later she turned, walking back towards the cottage very slowly. There was the faint sound of a car halting and the raucous cry of a cat and then all was still again, except for the perpetual whispering of the waves. With a heavy heart she opened the cottage door, sliding the bolts carefully behind her.

The fire was still on and in the dull golden glow she made her way across to the telephone. Jeff still did not reply and she put the receiver down slowly, feeling drained and empty. As she stood there, assailed by doubts, something else nudged at her consciousness. Beside the faint hiss of the fire and the subdued beat of the sea, there was another sound. She stiffened, the hair rising on the back of her neck. Unmistakably came the barely audible sound of light rapid breathing. And it wasn't her own.

Her heart began to beat in painful, erratic thumps and her hands were wet with sweat. She stood, her fingertips on the telephone receiver, rooted with fear. No one moved. Screwing up every ounce of courage she possessed, she turned her head slowly, her eyes straining into the darkness. Beyond the flickering shadows of the room she was in, lay the open doorway into the dining-room and kitchen. It gaped at her, a black hole with no chink of light, and from it came the disembodied breathing, the smell of someone else's presence.

If she could reach the outside door before him . . . but the bolts were on . . . Or the telephone . . . but he would be on her before the operator even answered . . . Dear God, she had to do *something!* She couldn't just stay here, rigid with fear like a rabbit waiting for the hounds. Perhaps if he thought she wasn't aware of his presence, if she behaved normally, went up to bed . . . perhaps he would let himself out . . .

She shrank with terror at the thought of moving towards the open door, of walking upstairs in the blackness, knowing he was only yards away, but if she didn't do something, he would know that she had heard him . . .

Her teeth bit into her lip so hard that she could taste blood. She held her breath, forcing herself to walk towards the dining-room, and the stairs that split the rooms in two. She could feel him stiffen, hear the breathing light and fast, and then she put her hand on the banister and began to climb upwards.

Then he moved. His hand caught the milk jug on the table, sending it crashing to the floor. She whirled round, hands outstretched for the light switch. But he was there before her.

With an oath, he grasped her wrist, wrenching her down the few stairs she had climbed, swinging her heavily against the door. The impact slammed all the breath out of her, knocking her half senseless. Then he was at the bolts, panting and swearing as he heaved them back. She struggled to her feet, clawing at the wall and the switch. He rounded on her, and she dodged behind the chair, then as he lunged towards her, she grasped the blanket, throwing it over him, crying with terror. He swore, falling heavily over the chair and she ran for the door, tugging at the bolt, but she wasn't quick enough. His arm closed round her, dragging her back into the room. She twisted and struggled, lashing out at him with her feet, and he let go with one hand, raising it and striking her with all his force on the side of the head. Blinded and semi-conscious, she reeled against the wall while he knocked the chair out of his way, making for the door. Desperately she pulled herself to her feet, reaching blindly for the switch. If she could only see him clearly, just for a minute . . .

The door swung open and then her fingers closed on the smooth metal. She pulled and the room was filled with bright, glaring light. He swore, and as he raised his hand to strike her she had a glimpse of a white face and eyes as terrified as her own. Then there was the gleam of metal and her skull seemed rent in a hundred pieces. From a far distance came the sound of a car engine and the black outline of a Jaguar past the window, rounding the sharp corner with a scream of brakes.

Whirling darkness engulfed her and her fingers lost their hold, sliding slowly down the wall until she lay in a blood-stained heap on the floor.

Chapter Fourteen

'There, there,' Mrs MacBride was crooning, pressing icy wet wads of cotton-wool against her head, which was cradled in her ample lap. Between flickering lashes Sally could see the familiar blue uniform of the police and as if from a great distance a male voice said impatiently: 'How much longer is the doctor goin' to be?'

'Hush now. Can you not see the lassie is comin' round? There, there, it's all right, everything is all right.'

Sally remained unconvinced as her vision blurred and the room swam in a dizzying vortex of lights and colour and strange faces. They backed away and other hands, cool and capable, moved her head gently, running over her body, lifting, feeling, pressing. Inertly she allowed herself to be handled, vaguely conscious of the doctor's voice questioning Mrs MacBride. She opened her eyes again and this time the weather-beaten face above hers remained solid and tangible.

'Can you talk, lass?'

She nodded, struggling to sit up, but he restrained her gently.

'You bide there a while. Now, what happened?'

While she spoke and the young policeman by his side wrote in his notebook, he continued to dress her scalp and she saw in mesmerized horror the handfuls of hair lying in a bloodied matted heap on the floor.

'And when you came into the cottage, you locked the door behind you?'

The young policeman's voice held a note of excitement, and Sally found herself smiling feebly: assaults and batteries wouldn't come his way very often in Islay. No doubt she made a change from traffic offences.

'Yes, the cottage has been broken into twice already and . . .'

'Just answer yes or no. There's no need to tire yourself. Had the room been disturbed?'

'Yes . . . I don't remember . . . No. No, it hadn't. I didn't put the light on but the fire was still on and I could see. I'm sure it was the same as when I left.'

The doctor began to circle her head with white bandage and then helped her slowly to sit up.

'And you said you managed to put the light on and that you saw him clearly?'

'Yes . . . he hit me and I fell against the wall and as he was pulling the bolts back . . . I managed to reach the switch just as he opened the door . . .'

'And . . .' the policeman prompted gently.

'He raised his hand . . . he had a gun . . .'

'And you saw him clearly?'

Her head was throbbing and the light hurt her eyes. She felt violently sick.

'You would be able to recognize him again?'

'Yes . . . no . . . I don't know. I'm sorry, I just don't know.'

'That's enough for now,' the doctor said firmly. 'Miss Craig will spend tonight in the hospital and you can speak to her again tomorrow.'

He turned to an ashen-faced Mrs MacBride. 'Perhaps you could collect some nightclothes for the lassie.'

A coat was laid gently around Sally's shoulders and at last she managed to say: 'Just how badly am I hurt, doctor?'

'Ach, it's lucky you are. Lucky. Only just caught you, the blow did. If you'd received the full impact from it, you'd be dead. Not a doubt of that. As it is, I dare say you'll be troubled by headaches for a wee while. Still, it's a small price to pay for such luck.' He smiled affably, helping her to her feet and supporting her with his arm and the help of the young policeman. 'You'll have a hangover as if it were Hogmanay tomorrow. But plenty of rest will help that and don't let Billy here wear you out with questions.'

'We need a description so that we can check on the ferries leavin' in the mornin',' Billy said doggedly.

'It was a Jaguar,' Sally said suddenly.

'You saw his car?' Billy asked, ignoring the doctor's glare.

'I must have . . . I don't remember how . . . but it was a Jaguar. I'm positive of it.'

She paused, puzzled, unable to remember any more.

'Don't worry, lass. He'll not be leavin' Islay, we'll see to that.'

Mrs MacBride hurried downstairs with a carrier bag, her face lined and anxious, and one of Billy's companions opened the door for them.

From under a night sky there came the everlasting thunder of the Atlantic swell and Sally said stupidly, 'But it's still night . . .'

'Ach, it's nearly half past three . . .'

'But I thought . . . it seemed ages . . . how . . .'

The doctor patted her arm reassuringly. 'Ye canna have been there for longer than fifteen minutes. Old Tom Gunn had been seein' to his lobster pots. When he passed An Cala the lights were blazin' and he could see right in. Dammity good thing he did as well.'

'Yes,' Sally murmured weakly, allowing herself to be helped into a car while Billy, the carrier bag clutched to his chest, squeezed in beside her.

'Leave the key with Constable Mackintosh,' he called out to Mrs MacBride as the car drove away, then, turning to Sally: 'We'll go over the place with a fine toothcomb tonight. Don't you worry, lassie. We'll get him, we'll get him.'

Her head hurt and she felt too weak to worry. Too weak to think any more. She was vaguely aware that she wanted to speak to Jeff but Jeff hadn't been in . . .

Passively she allowed herself to be led into the warmth of the hospital and put to bed gently and efficiently by a ward sister and nurse. In the morning she would be able to speak to Jeff, just now her head hurt too much to think, but in the morning . . . the nurse pulled the curtains and switched off the light. Joy ... she thought, as she sank into sleep ... joy cometh in the morning ...

She awoke, feeling stronger but with a fierce pain behind her eyes and though they brought a phone to her and let her telephone Jeff, it was no use. It rang and rang unanswered and she put the receiver down, blinking the tears away.

'The doctor will be seein' you about ten,' the nurse said, laying a tray of boiled eggs and toast in front of her. Sally didn't bother to reply. 'And there's a policeman to see you as soon as you've eaten.'

She toyed with the toast, unable to think about her attacker and whether he had been caught and who he was, unable to think of anything but Jeff.

The door opened again. 'A telegram for you. They've sent it on from Port Charlotte.'

She practically snatched it from the nurse's outstretched hands, opening it feverishly, the tea spilling into her saucer.

Flying to Paris stop Be with you soon stop Love you lots Jeff.

It had been sent at 6.15 the previous day. She leant back against the pillows with a sob of relief.

'Are you all right?' the nurse asked anxiously. 'I hope it wasn't bad news ...'

'No, it isn't bad news, it's good news. He's in Paris, you see, and I thought ...'

'Well, as it's good news,' the nurse said practically, 'perhaps you'll eat your eggs and toast. I'll get you a fresh cup of tea, you seem to have lost most of that.'

Even the pain behind her eyes seemed to have eased, and as she ate hungrily she allowed herself for the first time to speculate on what had happened to her. If nothing else, it proved her assumptions to be correct. The gun had been Miranda's and it had been for self-protection. But that wasn't what they were looking for. Whatever it was, Miranda had hidden it, and Miranda had wanted Sally, and Sally alone, to find it. Miranda had said Pete Mackay would explain what had been happening, and it looked as if Jeff would be seeing both Pete Mackay and Tony Carpenter today. With luck he might fly straight from Paris to Scotland: this time tomorrow he would probably be with her. Until then she would continue to ponder it out for herself.

'That's a lot better,' the nurse said, taking the empty plates away. 'The police have a few more questions . . .'

In as much detail as she could remember, Sally repeated what had happened the previous night. She also repeated her doubts as to Miranda's accidental drowning and the fact that the cottage had been broken into twice before. But she didn't mention the gun and she didn't mention Miranda's letter.

No Jaguar car had attempted to leave the island by the morning's ferry, and with the description that Sally felt able to give in the clear light of day, the local constabulary were quite optimistic that they would apprehend the men responsible. The doctor, too, was optimistic when he changed her dressing.

'As long as you take things gently, you'll come to no harm.'

'You mean I can leave?'

'Ach, it would do you good to stay and rest, but if you want to leave, I'll not stop you.'

'Oh thank you, doctor. I really do feel better this morning. It was mostly shock last night . . .'

'No wee headache?' he asked with a twinkle in his eyes.

She grinned. 'Now you come to mention it . . .'

'I'll give you some pain-killers, but I'll have to see you again. My surgery is in Sharples Street. I'll see you there tomorrow mornin' between nine and ten, and remember, no driving.'

'All right. I promise I'll behave myself and not do anything over-energetic.'

He laughed. 'That headache will see to that. It's a fine day. The fresh air and sun will do you good.'

He picked up his bag. 'Just one more thing, Miss Craig. I shouldn't stay at the cottage any more. Book into the hotel. Better safe than sorry, and until he's found . . .'

'Yes,' Sally said. 'I shall move to the hotel as soon as I leave the hospital. The police have insisted that I do.'

'Aye well, they're right. Good-day until tomorrow.'

The young nurse, who had helped put her to bed and who had brought her Jeff's telegram, now brought her clothes. As she dressed, she wondered for the first time how she would reach Port Charlotte without transport. Unless her memory was playing her tricks, it had been a good ten-minute drive last night to the hospital. She said hesitantly, 'You must think I'm awfully stupid, but where are we?'

The nurse looked up with raised eyebrows from the business of changing sheets. 'Bowmore. This is the only hospital on the island.'

'I see.'

'Can I help? You look worried.'

'I was just wondering how I would make my way back to Port Charlotte.'

'Ach, did he no' tell you?' She sniffed disparagingly. 'There's a policeman outside waitin' to take you back. He'll see you're all right.'

She hoped it would be the enthusiastic Billy but she was disappointed. Her chauffeur was a man of few words, and after a little while she gave up the task of making conversation and lapsed into silence.

The narrow road was now familiar. It led through lush farmland, down into the leafy dimness of the woods at Bridgend and out beside pools of sparkling water left behind by the tide. Very soon they were crossing open ground with flocks of grazing sheep and she noticed that the brilliant orange tent was still pitched there, though there was no sign of anyone about.

The sun shone down hotly and she was grateful when her companion opened his window half-way down. On this stretch of road there were no cottages or farms and very few trees. Thistle and steep banks of waving grasses grew thickly at the roadside, and everywhere over the grey-white rocks that strewed the shoreline were strands of gleaming seaweed, almost translucent beneath the heat of the sun. Strangely enough, she felt no anxiety at returning to Port Charlotte. The thought of leaving never entered her head.

The road skirted the jetty at Bruichladdich and in the distance she could see the whitewashed cottages of Port Charlotte, circled by screaming gulls. The policeman said suddenly, 'Sergeant Brady is waiting for you at the hotel.'

'But I've just spoken to someone, back at the hospital . . .' she said.

'Yes, miss, I know. But my instructions were to take you to the hotel and that Sergeant Brady would be meeting you there.'

She should have known what it would be about. Hadn't Billy told her quite clearly that they would search An Cala with a fine toothcomb? Her stomach muscles tightened. She should have told them everything. It wasn't likely that the fact that Miranda possessed a gun would find its way into the national press: she had acted over-cautiously. Now they would think she was not telling them the whole truth. For some ridiculous reason she felt guilty.

Sergeant Brady was very pleasant about it, and though she felt she was overdoing the explaining bit she couldn't stop herself.

'They printed such nasty things after her death—at least they were nasty as far as I and her parents were concerned. You know the sort of thing: Model and Lover in Suicide Pact? Miranda Taylor, ex-girl friend of Kings and Dukes, drowned in Hebrides. All a lot of nonsense. She only went out with him twice *and* he was an ex-King and had been for thirty years . . .'

'Miss Craig . . .'

'And I thought, if they get hold of the news that she had a gun with her they'll make her sound like a gangster's moll and so I didn't mention it, but it was really because I wasn't thinking straight anyway, and then . . .'

'Miss Craig,' the Sergeant said firmly, 'did Miss Taylor habitually carry a gun round with her?'

'No, of course not,' Sally said irritably. 'I've tried to explain to you once. She went to Turkey and after she came back her behaviour changed. Then she came here and days later she was dead . . . murdered.'

'Accidentally drowned.'

'Good grief, you can't still believe that!' Sally felt her control slipping away, but the Sergeant said sympathetically. 'Until we've proved otherwise, Miss Craig.'

'I'm sorry,' she said, suddenly deflated. 'But when you're so *sure* of something and no one will believe you, it's so . . .'

He patted her shoulder. 'Rest is what you need today. I'm quite sure that there was no deliberate attack on you. You disturbed him and he panicked. Islay isn't a big place, we'll have him soon enough.'

She smiled weakly. 'I'm sure you're right. If I thought otherwise I'd have left for home today. There's something at An Cala that somebody wants, but what . . .?'

The Sergeant shook his head. 'We found nothing last night, but it's not your worry, Miss Craig, it's ours. Leave it all to us.'

She wished she could, but the growing feeling that she was the only person who could solve the mystery was becoming an obsession. *We know each other so well that I don't have to put any more. I know you'll do what I want.* The sentence from Miranda's letter seemed to be branded with letters of fire into her brain.

After the Sergeant had handed over a easeful of her clothes and left her, she went to her new room at the hotel, putting her things away slowly, concentrating as hard as the pain in her head would allow her to. But it was no use. Whatever it was that Miranda would expect her to do, she couldn't for the life of her think of it.

Despairingly she made her way downstairs, hoping to find someone to talk to, but there was no sign of Mr and Mrs Rees and the lounge was empty except for an elderly gentleman in knee-length boots reading *The Oban Times*.

She strolled out into the brilliant sunlight, and began to walk seawards towards An Cala. She stood, gazing at the cottage for a long while, then, without attempting to go inside, walked across to her car and opened the door.

Her intention was simply to drive up the hill and park outside the hotel, but her head was feeling better and perversely she disobeyed the doctor's instructions and turned left at the hotel, driving at a sedate thirty-five miles an hour between the sprawling cottages of Port Charlotte and on to the high, narrow road with the sea pounding the rocks below and the air full of delicate spray and the purple and rust of the Rhinns of Islay spreading out before her.

A lump came to her throat as the road wound down to the shallow hump-backed bridge at Octoford and her heart and mind were so full of Jeff that it was a miracle she noticed the car at all. It wasn't until she reached Portnahaven, the southernmost point of the Rhinns, that she thought she was being followed, and even then it was only a faint suspicion.

She parked the car at the top of a steep lane bounded by a few derelict crofts and waited. Nothing happened. No one drove past. A cat swung its tail lazily, basking in the sun on a crumbling window-sill. Far below her was a small beach with a handful of boats hauled on to the sand, but there was no view of the road. She continued down the other side of the hill, dipping between farmed fields and then out on to the Rhinns again, the roadside thick with poppies, spreading like a crimson carpet over the misty purples of the moorland.

At the next corner and minutes later, the large Jaguar slid over the crest of the hill less than a hundred yards away from her.

Chapter Fifteen

Sally gripped the wheel tighter, her speed increasing. The Jaguar dropped rapidly back, until it was in the far distance, but it remained there, keeping her always in sight. The road grew steeper and narrower and her hands on the wheel began to shake. She must get back to Port Charlotte and Sergeant Brady. She raced down an incline, along an uneven stretch of rough cobble, round another bend . . .

Then, like a shaft of light, she knew there was no need to panic. It wasn't her he was after. He could have caught up with her any time, and where better than in this, the most isolated and lonely part of the island?

He was using her. He couldn't find what he was looking for by himself, and he was hoping that she would lead him to it. Her spirits soared. She opened the window, breathing in deeply. Two could play at that game. If she could turn the tables and follow *him*, then she'd really have something to tell the police.

The ground grew rougher and stonier and soon her speed was down to twenty miles an hour and then fifteen, but always, in the far distance, was the dark speck of the Jaguar. She wondered if this was the first time she had been followed or if it had been happening ever since she'd landed on the island. There was no way of telling, but one thing was for sure: if he was going to follow her back to the hotel and wait in the vicinity for her leaving, the police would soon pick him up. The thought did not fill her with the elation it should have. The idea of turning the tables and following him had appealed to her. Somewhere in the far recesses of her mind she could hear Jeff muttering 'Stupid, silly . . .' and he was probably right. All the same . . .

She came to a turning for Octoford and veered down it. The track was so overgrown that there was only just room for the tyres between the high grass. The moors stretched out on all sides as far as the eye could see, an unending vista of russets and olive green. Not until the turning was nearly out of sight did the Jaguar follow after. She smiled grimly to herself, as the car rolled and heaved over the uneven ground. In the distance she caught the quick, bright gleam of the sea, and minutes later the cliffs came into view and the track dropped down to join the road from Port Charlotte to Portahaven.

He was still behind her as she approached Port Charlotte. She gripped the wheel tighter, overcome by a wave of rising excitement, a half-formed plan already in her head. With growing satisfaction she saw that Mr Rees's car was parked outside the front of the hotel and she drove slowly past, continuing down the short, steep street to the sea, and parking in her usual place outside An Cala. Then she locked the doors and strolled nonchalantly back towards the hotel.

There was no sign anywhere of the pursuing car but she felt quite sure that her actions were being watched by someone, somewhere. At least she hoped they were.

She found Mr Rees alone in the lounge, busily taking down notes from one of his books.

'What the . . .' he began, staring at her bandaged head.

'An accident,' she said hurriedly. 'It's really not so bad as it looks.'

He continued to stare, his expression doubtful. 'Looks pretty bad to me. What on earth were you doing? Not in the car, I hope?'

She laughed. 'I'm too careful a driver for that. I was wondering actually if you could do me a favour?'

He put down his pen and notebook, beaming good-naturedly. 'Anything, anything. Your wish is my command. Another visit to Dunyvaig perhaps . . .'

She sat on the edge of the chair opposite him. 'It's an awful cheek, really, but I wonder . . .' She hesitated uncomfortably.

'No need to be shy. Now what is it? It can't be so drastic.'

'I was wondering perhaps if I could borrow your car this evening. You see mine's kaput and I had arranged to go somewhere which is important to me, and . . .'

'Tut, child, is that all it is? I thought at least you were going to ask for the Crown jewels.' He fumbled in his jacket pocket for his car keys. 'Here they are. I've no need to tell you to drive carefully, I know you will. Would you like a coffee before you go? I was just about to order some.'

'No, thanks awfully, I must rush. And thank you again for the car.'

She left him, filling his pipe and gazing after her with a shadow of concern in his eyes. Hurriedly she went to her room, changed her dress and slipped a lightweight coat over the top, tied a headsquare over her hair, pulling it forwards so that it hid the tell-tale white of her bandage, then put on a pair of sunglasses. Not exactly what the best-dressed woman of the year would wear, but it would do for what she wanted. Then, with her heart thumping painfully in her chest, she strolled out to Mr Rees's car and slid behind the steering wheel.

Slowly she reversed out into the road, her eyes straining left and right for a glimpse of the Jaguar. The only other car was a Mini making deliveries to the village shop, and she turned right towards Bridgend, scanning every turning and every yard for sight of the incriminating car. By the time she reached Bruichladdich without any sign of him, her hopes were fading. She turned, continuing back to Port Charlotte, past the hotel and out on to the road she had travelled earlier, but without any luck. She reversed again, and as she approached the village for the second time, noticed that the cottages that lined the main street were flanked by long gardens and then a row of garages, and the garages were a good six feet higher in level than the houses. It was possible that from that height a person could see quite clearly down on to the hotel.

A steep path led between two of the houses to the garages, but Sally did not attempt to drive up. If her suspicions were correct, there would be too little room for the two of them there. Instead, she parked outside the shop, went inside and bought a bar of chocolate and some sweets, and then casually walked up between the steeply rising gardens to the line of garages. She hadn't reached half-way when she saw the nose of the Jaguar poking out from the end of one of the garages. Hardly able to suppress her elation she turned quickly, hurrying back towards the car. All the time she sat there, waiting for him to make a move, she knew she should have been on her way to the police, but the longing to have some of the glory for herself, especially in Jeff's eyes, was too strong. She stayed where she was, drumming her fingers on the wheel in nervous anticipation.

An hour went by—two. The sun was beginning to move westwards towards the steely grey horizon and the clouded hills beyond Loch Indaal. She yawned, wondering if perhaps she wasn't quite as clever as she'd thought, and if he knew she was waiting for him.

Just then a Range Rover eased its way into the street behind her. The doors slammed and a tall young man bounded across the pavement and up the path. Her heart began to thump again and she took firm hold of the wheel, her body tense and ready to move. Minutes later, the man who had attacked her ran lightly down into the main street, opened the door of the Range Rover and was speeding past her without a second glance.

Firmly she counted to twenty and then pressed her foot lightly down on the accelerator and began to follow. Her intentions were perfectly clear in her own mind. When she had tailed him to where he was staying, she would hot-foot it directly to the police station and lay the information triumphantly before them. Whatever Jeff found out from Pete Mackay in Paris, at least she would have done her bit.

He drove swiftly through Bruichladdich and round the head of the loch. She hung back as far as possible, so far in fact that she almost lost him. She actually passed the turning to Sanaigmore and was continuing on to Bridgend when she realized that he was no longer in front of her. Anxiously she swung the car round, speeding down the only turning he could have gone down. Five minutes later she breathed a sigh of relief. He was in front of her, driving as fast as the narrow road would allow. She had brought neither maps nor guide-book with her and racked her brains to keep her sense of direction and reconstruct in her head the lay-out of the island. If she remembered rightly, this turning cut across the narrowest part of the island, to where Loch Gruinart bit deeply inland. She couldn't remember any villages being close by ...

Once again she nearly lost him. This time it was sheer chance that she happened to catch a glimpse of the car bucketing down a rough track that led off from the right. There was no signpost and she hesitated, wondering if this was where her detective work came to an end and if the track led only to a farm.

Nervously she followed, going very slowly. She passed a large, stone-built farm standing in a circle of trees a short distance from the track, but there was no sign of any parked car, and as she peered through the windscreen she could see that fresh tyre marks led onwards. With a deep breath she pressed her foot down again gently. She had been right in her sense of direction. To the left of her stretched the desolate shores of Loch Gruinart: the tide was out and the sand was damp and bleak-looking, soggy clumps of grass and scrub grew among hollows of sand still filled with the receding sea water. The wind from the sea blew coldly, waving the tall rushes at the roadside like a field of corn, and a flock of gulls skimmed across the shallow surface of the water, fluttering down to an outcrop of jagged rock.

Abruptly she halted. In the distance was another farm or cottage, and the car was stationary outside it. She had been so immersed in the view and the beauty of the birds flying down against the steely grey sky that she had nearly followed him into his own back garden. There wasn't another house in sight. The cottage was protected from the harsh Atlantic winds by a screen of high privet, and beyond it the sand dunes ran out to the point and the open sea. Behind it was rolling grassland and a handful of grazing sheep and nothing else but sky and cloud.

With a sigh of satisfaction she reversed the car, heading back with her news to Sergeant Brady and the warmth of the hotel lounge.

She had only got as far as the junction with the main road when the Range Rover bore down behind her. She gazed stupidly in the mirror as it approached at high speed and she just had time to turn left towards Port Charlotte, her feet manipulating accelerator and clutch in a state of frozen horror, when he overtook her.

She stared unbelievably as he speeded away down the deserted road. The man at the wheel wasn't her attacker. It was Tony Carpenter.

Chapter Sixteen

'What the . . .' she began, then pushed her own foot down, racing after him before he should disappear altogether.

Heedless of the bumpy road and the protesting shudders from the car, she sped determinedly on, back to the coast road and the sight of the sun slipping down beyond the rim of the bay. She was just in time to see the gleam of his car turn right and minutes afterwards screamed round the corner, nearly running into the back of him.

To all intents and purposes he was enjoying the view. A cigarette was held lightly in the long fingers and he was gazing across the silver surface of the sea as if he had no other thought on his mind than to wonder what time dinner would be served. She ground to a halt behind him and flung open her door.

With a barely perceptible turn of the head he leant across and opened the far door of his car.

Trembling with fury and indignation she slammed it behind her.

'What the bloody hell do you think you're playing at?' she demanded. Then, not waiting for a reply: 'I think I'm at least owed an explanation for this.' She pointed to her bandaged head which was throbbing more painfully with every passing minute.

He raised a protesting hand, showing not the slightest surprise at her presence or her outburst.

'My dear Sally, you have my heartfelt apologies. It was an accident, a terrible mistake . . .'

'*An accident!*' she began, her voice rising. 'An *accident*. How . . .'

'I am well aware that a lot of explanations are owed to you, and I can't make them while you're shouting at me.'

'It's been you who has been breaking into the cottage and . . .'

He nodded. 'True, true, but you've yet to hear the reason *why*. When you do, you will view things in a different light.'

'I can hardly wait,' she said bitterly, the blood pounding behind her eyes.

He leant back, utterly at ease, the only expression on his face one of deep concern. 'It's too long a story to tell here. Let's drive on to Port Charlotte and talk in the comfort of the bar.'

'What about your friend?'

He raised an eyebrow slightly.

'The one parked behind the garages and waiting for me to make my exit from the same hotel. Won't he be getting a little tired by now?'

'A good point. It would seem he is wasting his time.' He blew a mouthful of smoke into the air, then turned, leaning towards her.

'We don't know each other very well, Sally, but believe me, there is a very good reason for all that has happened. Follow me in your car and let's talk about it.'

She hesitated. There was something in his manner that was convincing, and what alternative had she?

With bad grace she flounced out of the Range Rover and into her own.

She had plenty of time to think as they covered the now familiar road back to Port Charlotte, but none of her thoughts made much sense. On the surface Tony Carpenter seemed likeable enough, and at least he was going to explain to her. 'It had better be good,' she murmured to herself. 'It had better be good, or else . . .'

Or else she would report both him and his unpleasant friends to the police: in point of fact she would probably do that anyway, but she wanted to hear his 'explanation' first.

He drove leisurely round the head of the bay and down among Port Charlotte's cottages. He was standing outside the hotel ready to open her car door for her when she pulled up beside him. As she did so, he looked above and beyond her, and waved his arm with an outstretched hand. She didn't deign to look in the same direction, but walked with as much dignity as she could muster into the hotel's bar. It was quite crowded, but mercifully there was no sign of Mr and Mrs Rees. Sally had no wish to be interrupted. She sat in a corner and waited for Tony to bring the drinks over. Whatever happened now, she was at least within the familiar walls of the hotel and the fact was immensely comforting.

He sat opposite her, waiting silently until she had finished half her drink, and then he said in a voice charged with emotion, 'I am most damnably sorry for what happened last night.'

She remained silent, and he put his glass on the table with a long, drawn-out sigh. 'It all began,' he said quietly, 'in Turkey.'

She looked up, staring directly at him, recognizing the truth when she heard it. She dared not speak. He said, his eyes still holding hers, 'It all began with Miranda and that cursed trip to Ani.'

There was a long silence. He ran a finger lightly round the rim of his glass and said slowly, 'What I am going to tell you, Sally, you are not going to like. But I want you to promise me one thing. Hear me out.'

She nodded, not taking her eyes away from his, the muscles of her stomach contracting painfully, her mouth dry and parched.

'Miranda was a good friend of yours and this will be painful for you, but it's the truth, so help me, it's all the truth.'

There were no mannerisms now. If ever a man was serious and had his mind on what he was saying, Tony Carpenter had at that moment.

'You probably remember that party at Jeff Roberts' place. That was the first time I met Miranda. She told me she was flying out to Turkey to do some modelling and I saw it as a heaven-sent opportunity to get my Range Rover back—my brother had been out there for some time and showed no sign of returning home. I asked her quite casually, I had no idea . . .' His voice faded and the blue eyes clouded.

'And . . .' she prompted, hardly able to bear the suspense.

He took another sip of his drink. 'She said yes, it was fine by her. She wanted a short time to herself, it couldn't have come at a better time.' He shrugged his shoulders expressively. 'They were together out there for several weeks . . .'

'Miranda and your brother?'

He nodded. 'Yes. He's older than me by six years. Anyway, there they were . . . and the inevitable happened. Scott believed it was the real thing and, as people do, confidences were shared and he told her too much . . . and wrote too much.'

'I . . . don't understand.'

'You will,' he said quietly. 'Unfortunately he told her a lot about other people . . . a lot about myself. You may not know it, but I'm unofficially engaged to Marisa St John. Her father, being a Duke, didn't go a great bundle on me as a prospective son-in-law, but it was coming along nicely. He'd mellowed considerably and the engagement was to be announced on Marisa's twenty-first birthday party.'

'What has this to do with Miranda?' Sally asked.

'Scott wrote to her when she left and got no reply so he flew to London. They had a row and Miranda became . . .' He hesitated, then continued. 'She became petty.' He took a deep breath. 'She said she would make him sorry and regret that he ever knew her. Well, she did that all right. She had Scott's letters and in them were some things about myself that I would prefer people didn't know. She said she would show them to Marisa's father.'

Sally stared, unable to take in what Tony was revealing. The silence lengthened. At last she said, 'I'm sorry. I don't understand what you're saying.'

'I'm saying,' he said flatly, 'that Miranda was so peeved when Scott broke off the affair that she threatened to get her own back by ruining any chance of my marriage with Marisa St John.'

White-faced and trembling, Sally said, 'That's impossible. Miranda would never stoop to such a thing and why should she? She was one of the most beautiful girls in London, she could have had any man she wanted. Why should she want your brother?'

'I don't know,' Tony said frankly. 'Perhaps she didn't, but she didn't want him to be the one to finish with her, which is what he

128

did. She wasn't used to that sort of treatment. The only way she could hit back was through me. She knew how Scott would feel if, because of his foolishness, I was made to suffer. I'll be perfectly honest with you, Sally. Marrying Marisa was the greatest thing that could happen to me. Besides being a damn nice girl, she's heiress to a fortune. Miranda knew the weight behind her threat, believe you me. She told Scott to think it over, that she was coming up here for a few days and that she'd post the incriminating letters from Islay, unless he got in touch with her to the contrary.'

He gulped down the rest of his drink. 'The bloody thing is, Scott didn't matter to her. She was just peeved, wilful and spoilt. It was nothing more than getting her own back ... Scott didn't think she'd do it, but I asked Gregory, and Gregory said sure as hell she'd do it. That's why he and Scott came here. He was the only friend I had who was a friend of hers as well. He said he'd try and talk some sense into her ...'

'And Scott took her walking out at Octoford.'

'I beg your pardon?'

'Nothing,' Sally said wearily. 'They were seen and I couldn't imagine who the man was, that's all.'

There was silence for a little while and then she said in a low voice, 'And the drowning?'

'An accident. Gregory wasn't such a good swimmer. What really happened is as much a mystery to me as it is to you. Gregory did suffer from epilepsy though. It's possible he had an attack and Miranda tried to save him ... but I needed Scott's letters back.'

'What was in them must have been awfully defamatory,' Sally said numbly.

'Even in these permissive days it would be what you call defamatory. If Marisa had got to know of it I doubt if she would have married me anyway, and if her father had got to know ... So Dave came to Islay to help Scott look for the letters.'

Sally was dimly aware that he left the table for fresh drinks, but she was lost in her personal hell and was hardly aware when he returned. After a while she said, 'But the cottage was broken into *before* Miranda and Gregory were drowned.'

'That was Gregory. Miranda thought it a huge joke when he arrived, intent on saving my honour and she had no intention of either handing the letters over or destroying them, so Gregory chanced his arm . . .'

'I see. And Pete Mackay?'

'Who?'

'Miranda wrote to me saying Pete Mackay would explain everything to me.'

'That *Pete Mackay* would?'

They stared at each other and Sally said slowly, 'You're supposed to be in Paris with him now. Jeff's gone to see you both . . .'

'The name Pete Mackay,' Tony said, 'means nothing to me at all.'

Sally leaned weakly back in her chair. 'Jeff phoned you from here, right?'

'Right. That's why I decided to come. I told him Gregory and Miranda had been having an affair in the hope that it would stop him interfering any more.'

'And you told him that Miranda still had some belongings in Gregory's flat?'

'Right again. I knew the letters weren't there, I saw no harm in Roberts collecting them.'

'Jeff left the next morning for London and phoned me later saying he'd been to see you, and a friend of yours at your flat said you'd left for Paris with Pete Mackay and wouldn't be back till Friday.'

Tony stared at her. 'Friend? What friend? My flat is locked up and empty.'

Sally raised a hand to her throbbing head and Tony said, 'Is Jeff Roberts coming back here?'

She nodded.

'And just what *is* it he's looking for?'

Sally closed her eyes. 'He's looking for Pete Mackay. Miranda wrote me this letter the day before the drowning. She said if anything happened to her, Pete Mackay would explain. That's why we came.'

'I see,' he said slowly. 'Well, all I can suggest is that we wait for him to return and give us an explanation. I've never heard the name before. He always did have a jealous disposition.'

'I beg your pardon?' Sally stiffened.

'Roberts. That's why he's here, isn't it? Thought Miranda had been playing around behind his back . . . You want to be careful where he is concerned. He's not to be trusted.'

She felt suddenly very tired, too tired to think any more.

'Dave, that's the friend who came with Scott, he decided to have just one more search the other night. The letters must be in An Cala *somewhere*. He lost his head when you walked in . . . Dear God'—he buried his head in his hands. 'When he told us what had happened I knew I had to see you, to explain . . . but I daren't just walk in on you in case you called the police before I had a chance to speak to you. If you still want to call them I don't blame you, not after what Dave did . . . but if what I've told you tonight gets into the papers, it will just be as bad as if Miranda had carried out her threats . . .'

She shook her head, her heart heavy within her chest, her throat so constricted that she could hardly speak. 'I don't want anything else in the papers . . .'

'Thank God for that! Then it's over. We can forget it.'

She raised her head. 'There are still the letters—and Pete Mackay.'

He looked directly at her. 'You haven't got them?'

'No, there's nothing at An Cala. I don't believe Miranda still had them. You didn't know her very well. She *was* wilful, but she would never have carried out her threats. She was teasing Scott, tormenting him, but she would never have kept the letters in order to use them.'

'You really believe that?'

'I do. She never kept any correspondence. You've nothing to fear . . .'

He leant back in his chair, his eyes momentarily closed. 'But she told Pete Mackay.'

'I don't know that she did. She just said that he could explain.'

'*Someone* is going to have to explain *something*,' Tony said grimly.

'We'll just have to wait for Jeff. I'm expecting him back tomorrow or the day after.'

'He's sure going to be mad as hell when he sees that!' Tony said, referring to her head. 'I think it would be best if we didn't stop around to meet him. Not till he's had the chance to cool down. All I can ask, Sally, is that you accept my apologies for all that's happened and let me know about this Pete Mackay business.'

'Why the book?' she asked suddenly, as he rose to leave.

He frowned. 'Book? What book?'

'Norman Mailer's *Marilyn*. It was taken from the cottage after it had been broken into.'

He smiled. 'Blame Scott. I'll have him return it. He's an avid Monroe fan.'

She watched him leave, her head aching viciously. She had wanted an explanation and she had got it. More, she'd had her doubts about Jeff rekindled. Wretchedly she rose to her feet and made her way towards her room and her bed, yearning for the blessed release of sleep, to forget, however temporarily, what she had been told, to pretend none of it had ever happened.

Chapter Seventeen

She slept soundly and deeply and when she woke it was to an azure blue sky and the sight of gulls soaring and wheeling over the harbour wall. She rolled over, the nerves in her stomach tightening as she remembered the previous night. Resolutely she thrust it to the back of her mind; dwelling on it would do her no good whatsoever, Jeff would be here soon, and with his coming the heavy weight that seemed to be weighing her down, would lift and disappear.

She dressed quickly, anxious to be among people, to talk idly about the weather and the scenery, anything that would prevent her mind from returning to her conversation with Tony Carpenter.

The day was unusually hot for September. A soft breeze blew in from the sea, and Sally ate breakfast by an open window, grateful for the refreshing tang of the pure air. Across the bay the distant hills were sharp and clear against the cloudless sky. It was a perfect day for walking . . . if you had company.

She glanced at her watch, trying to remember what time the early ferry from the mainland landed, hoping against hope that Jeff was on board. If she hurried her breakfast, she would be just in time to meet it . . .

She forgot all about her promise to be at the doctor's surgery, her only thought that of seeing Jeff again.

There was no sign of Mr Rees and so she left his car keys with the receptionist and walked quickly out into the sunshine. The steep street to An Cala was filled with children playing and the sound of their shouts and laughter went a little way towards making her feel better. It was all a misunderstanding. Tony had believed that Miranda would ruin his life out of petty spite, and so he and his friends had acted as they had. Whereas Sally knew, without a shadow of doubt, that Miranda would have done no such thing. She had simply been tormenting Scott Carpenter and probably hardly gave the matter a second's thought. An unbidden question asked: But why then had she written the letter?

She stood frowning, hand on the door of the car, staring at the white-capped waves as they rolled ceaselessly shorewards. The niggle became a doubt as she drove out on the coast road and headed towards Port Askaig. Despairingly she brought the car to a halt at the roadside and delved in her shoulder-bag for the letter. For the hundredth time she read it through. Coupled with what Tony had told her, there wasn't really anything strange about it. Apart from the identity of Pete Mackay. Miranda had obviously realized she had behaved badly, that was all.

Sally stuffed the letter back. All this speculation had to stop, her head felt as if it were about to burst, and she was making herself physically ill and mentally depressed by it all. Miranda was dead. Nothing she could do would alter that. The time had come when she should put the affair out of her mind, before it consumed her completely.

Having made a decision, she felt better, and even began to hum as she drove past the glittering surface of a deserted loch, on towards Port Askaig.

As she rounded the last corner that led to the harbour, she saw that the ferry was just docking and her heart was in her mouth as she scanned the handful of passengers already disembarking. There was no mistaking that dark head of hair. The relief was nearly unbearable. All doubts of him vanished. He was here, that was all that mattered. She sped down the hill, tyres squealing as she halted abruptly at the tiny quayside, her heart and mind so full of him that she didn't notice the worried lines about his mouth or the tiredness of his eyes.

She called his name loudly, dodging between holiday-makers and their luggage, and crates of whisky waiting to be shipped back to the mainland.

'Jeff! Jeff! Thank goodness! Oh, I'm so glad to see you . . .'

He caught her in his arms and kissed her firmly on the mouth.

'We . . . ell, this *is* a welcome for the homecoming hero.'

'If you knew how much I've *missed* you . . .'

His hands tightened on her arms and he pushed her away suddenly, staring at her bruised and swollen forehead.

'What the hell have you done?'

'It's a long story, but there's no need to look so cross. I'm all right, really. You should have seen me yesterday when I was swathed in bandages. I took them off this morning in order to look my best for you!' She wriggled back into the circle of his arms. 'Oh Jeff, it's so good to have you back. It felt as though you were away for weeks.'

'It's good to be back, sweetheart. But first things first. I want to know how you did that?'

'And I want to know about Paris and Pete Mackay.'

He groaned. 'Of all the futile wastes of time that beat the lot. Let me get my car, then we'll talk.'

His car was not his car at all and Sally stared at it in surprise. He laughed. 'You don't think I've travelled via London, do you? If I had I'd still be on my way. I flew direct to Edinburgh from Paris and hired this at the airport.'

'If we hurry back to the hotel we can park one of the cars and share the other, it's bound to be friendlier!'

He squeezed her shoulders. 'You're a beloved half-wit, Sally Craig, but I missed you.'

With her spirits soaring, and Tony's remarks pushed to the back of her mind, Sally followed him up the steep hill and out towards the moors. The sun shone down on the glossy leaves of the trees, and the blue of the harebells that grew at the roadside. Everything seemed to sparkle and shine, from the rushing water of the burns to the gleaming wing tips of the birds as they darted low across the road in front of them. It was a beautiful day, and the cares of the last few weeks slipped from Sally's shoulders, making her feel almost giddy with relief.

Mr Rees passed them as they headed towards Port Charlotte.

He pressed his hand on his car horn, tooting loudly and waving and beaming, while Mrs Rees smiled shyly, looking half-apologetic for her husband's good humour. Sally waved energetically back, hoping to reassure him that any worries he may have had about her, had been needless. Still tooting, he disappeared in a cloud of dust down an unsignposted side road.

Happily Sally followed Jeff into Port Charlotte's narrow streets and to the hotel. He opened the car door for her with a flourish, his finger on his lips.

'Not a word until we're comfortably seated and I've drunk at least two cups of coffee.'

Hand in hand they went into the deserted lounge, sitting in the same place that Sally had been sitting in when he first walked in on her, six days ago. The little waitress was obviously delighted at Jeff's return, and the coffee came quickly, hot and strong, with a little silver jug of cream. When he had drunk his promised two cups he turned to her, and there was an expression in his eyes that Sally couldn't make out.

'And now, Sally, I want to know how you did that.'

'I didn't. Someone else did.'

'Don't tease me, Sal. What happened?'

'Well, as someone else said to me not so very long ago, do me one favour. Hear me out.'

'I'll wring your neck if you don't start talking sense,' Jeff said grimly.

She laughed. 'Just remember that the end of the story explains the beginning.'

'Sally . . .' he began dangerously.

'All right, I'll begin. The evening after you left I was talking to Mrs MacBride, telling her I was leaving actually, and she mentioned that there is an outside loo at An Cala and so I went to have a look at it.' She had begun talking quite spiritedly, but now she hesitated . . . 'And I found a gun wrapped in polythene, hidden in the cistern.'

She stopped altogether, her face paling, then she said in a whisper, 'Oh, my God! What a fool I've been! The gun . . .'

He grasped her wrist tightly. 'What *is* it, Sally? What's the matter?'

She began to tremble, talking more to herself than to Jeff and certainly making no sense to him.

'He explained everything and it seemed to fit. It *did* fit, but I forgot about the gun. If what he said was true, why should Miranda have had the gun?'

Struggling for self-control, Jeff said, 'For God's sake, Sally, *explain.*'

Her head was beginning to throb again and she struggled to get her thoughts in order. She told him what had happened from the time she had found the gun to her meeting with Tony Carpenter and his explanation for being there and for the break-ins at An Cala and the assault on her. She told him that Tony Carpenter did not know a Pete Mackay and that there had been no one in his flat who could possibly have given Jeff the message about his being in Paris with Pete Mackay. She didn't look at him while she was talking. Her hand was imprisoned in his and she kept her eyes on the table in front of them, concentrating so that she would get everything in its right order and not miss anything out. Not until she finished did she raise her head to look directly at him.

If she had ever thought she had seen Jeff Roberts look angry in the past, it was nothing to what he looked now; his mouth twisted and he said viciously, 'And I fell for it, going on that bloody stupid trip to Paris . . .'

She said, worried at the expression on his face, 'But you're here now, Jeff, and we can still go to the police . . .'

'You bet we can. Right now. But it will be too late, Sally. Those bastards will be gone by now.'

'You . . . think I was taken in?' Sally asked, knowing the answer.

He nodded grimly. 'There may be a shred of truth in what he told you, but not much. It hardly explains why Miranda had the gun hidden, or why I was sent on a wild goose chase out of the way. It smells to high heaven.'

She said with a catch in her voice, 'But they still haven't found what they were looking for . . . the letters . . .'

'Not letters, Sally. That story sounds a little too trite. But looking for something, and now they know as much as we do. That the person with the explanations is Pete Mackay.'

It was becoming so complicated and Sally wondered how much more she could take. Suspicion was everywhere.

'What happened in Paris?' she asked wearily.

'When I got to the address the fellow at Carpenter's flat gave me, no one had heard of him. And there was no reply when I rang back for an explanation.'

She drew in her breath. 'So we're back to square one. Miranda said Pete Mackay would explain, and Pete Mackay cannot be found.'

He stood up, pulling her to her feet. 'First things first, Sally. Let's see the police, and if they don't catch up with them I promise you one thing: I will. Sometime, somewhere, I'll catch up with them.'

His voice was quiet and hard, and Sally felt her spine prickle.

Only her head wound prevented the local constabulary from taking a very serious view of her behaviour in not getting in touch with them the previous evening. She told them that she hadn't been able to think clearly, which was true enough, but by the time they emerged into the strong light of midday she felt criminally negligent.

Sergeant Brady had been more than plain-spoken, warning them to do no amateur detective work on their own and to inform the police of anything that might occur in the future, no matter how trivial it seemed. They promised not to leave Islay for at least forty-eight hours and even Sally was lulled into a false sense of security by Jeff's apparent reasonableness and politeness. She should have known better.

'We'll give them an hour to check the farm out and see if they're still there,' he said, once they were alone, 'and if the answer is no and there's been no trace of them leaving the island, we'll start our own little hunt.'

'Do you think we ought to, Jeff?' she asked in a small voice.

He was emphatic. 'Yes, I think the police are just treating this as a case of assault by a burglar caught in the act, but it's more than that, Sally, much more. If you don't feel up to it, stay at the hotel and rest—it's what you should be doing anyway.'

'No, thank you, I've had too much of being by myself. Wherever you're going, I'm going too.'

He grinned. 'That means Port Askaig.'

'*Again?*' Sally asked unbelievingly.

'We know the three of them didn't leave by the early morning ferry. I want to check out the lunchtime one, and the airport at well.'

'But, Jeff,' she protested weakly, 'surely the police will do that?'

'I want to do it for my own satisfaction. Besides, there's always the chance I may meet up with the bastard who did that to you. And that would make my day.'

Chapter Eighteen

They were in time to see the ferry sail, and there was no Tony Carpenter on board, nor the man who had attacked her, and neither of the cars she had seen them use. Jeff didn't waste time, he swung the car round, speeding down the arrow-straight road that led across a vast expanse of peat and heather to the island's tiny airport. On either side of them wild bog cotton hung silver heads beneath the light drizzle that fell steadily.

Sally remained in the car, staring dejectedly at the greyness and desolation that surrounded her, while Jeff made his enquiries. Her main worry was that they *would* find them, since she had no doubt as to what would happen if Jeff came within striking distance of the man who had hit her. She hoped they were far away by now: as far as she was concerned, the police could handle the matter and the less she was involved the better.

Jeff ran back to the car, wiping the damp from his face and his hair as he said, 'Not a blasted thing. Which means they're still here, somewhere. Where did you say the farm was?'

It was useless to protest. Once again they rounded the head of Loch Indaal, once again Sally left the main road for the windy track that led to the lonely shores of Loch Gruinart and to the farmhouse.

The track girdled the water's edge as they made their way further and further out on to the point. Sally looked behind them. There was not another house in sight, nothing at all but the steely grey surface of the loch and the high, banking clouds, and the moors stretching endlessly into the distance.

Jeff passed the place where she had stopped the previous day, and as the farm drew nearer, she eyed it apprehensively. It was well built and sturdy, sitting squarely before the loch's edge, impervious to the Atlantic winds that beat at it almost continuously. Only the adjoining buildings had fallen prey to the weather and their walls were open to the sky, their crumbling interiors filled with rubble and climbing weeds. Jeff forced the car over the rough ground at the side of the house and, to Sally's unspeakable relief, she caught a glimpse of a navy uniform behind the small paned windows in their deep, almost medieval embrasures.

Jeff saw it too. 'Damn and blast . . .'

'Let's go, Jeff. We shouldn't have come, they won't be very pleased.'

'Rubbish. It gives us the opportunity of finding out what they've done so far.'

Before she could try to persuade him to change his mind the door opened and a policeman emerged from the dim light. Jeff was out of the car and across to meet him before Sally had been able to open her door. She sighed, changing her mind, and sat back, watching.

The wind whistled angrily round the car, tossing the knee-deep grass in front of the house into a waving mass of green, as the two men stood on the doorstep of the house, talking. The policeman, unlike his colleagues in Port Charlotte, seemed gregarious and quite pleased at Jeff's arrival. She could see Jeff's hands moving descriptively as he explained who he was and why he was there, and the policeman looked across at the car, nodding his head to her and then turning once more to Jeff, lips pursed and an expression of sympathy and concern on his face.

With what appeared to be friendly goodbyes he went back into the house and Jeff hurried back to the car.

He said breathlessly, 'The place was empty when the police got here. They must have cleared out as soon as Carpenter got back from seeing you. The farmhouse is only used as a holiday cottage, the owners haven't received the key back yet.' He paused. 'So we have the rest of the island to take our pick from. They're still here somewhere, but where?'

'To tell you the truth, Jeff,' Sally said in a low voice, 'I don't really care.'

He stared at her in surprise.

She said with a rush, 'What I'd really like to do, Jeff, is to go home. I'm tired of it all. Let's leave it to the police now . . .'

'And Miranda?'

She twisted the ring on her little finger and then said slowly, 'I don't believe we will find out any more. Whatever it was that so disturbed her in the last few weeks will have to remain a mystery. At least I have the satisfaction of knowing I did my best. I guess I'm just not detective material.'

His arm slid along the back of her neck, circling her shoulders, pulling her close. 'If that's how you feel, Sally, we'll drop the whole thing.'

'Really?' she said, turning to him, her spirits rising.

'There's no point if it's causing you worry . . .'

'And we'll go back to London?'

'Yes. But we'll have to tell Sergeant Brady. We promised we'd stay here at least another forty-eight hours, remember?'

She leant back. 'I may regret it in the future, but I really want to go home. I feel as if . . . whatever we find . . . is going to be nasty and unpleasant . . . and I don't want anything to spoil my memories of Miranda.'

'You're a goose, Sal,' he said, his voice thick as his lips came down on hers.

A few seconds later he pushed her gently away, his hands on her shoulders, staring straight at her, and as if he were a thought reader, he said gravely, 'You still don't have any doubts about Miranda and myself, do you?'

'No,' she said, meaning it, sure now in his presence that her suspicions were false. 'Whatever you tell me, I believe.'

'Will you promise always to stay with me.'

'I promise.'

Despite the persistent drizzle and the cold wind it was an afternoon that Sally was always to look back on as golden. They lunched at the Machrie Hotel on grilled lobster seasoned with a pâté that had a mysterious flavour of malt whisky, then they climbed hand in hand over the steep dunes and the short, springy turf to the sea. They gazed at the immense sweep of the bay in front of them: mile after mile of pure, unsullied sand lay open to the pounding Atlantic. Huge breakers thundered on the deserted shore, the spray from the surf stinging their cheeks and their lips as they ran heedlessly downwards to the untrodden silver sand.

They left their shoes behind them, racing into the surging shallows, laughing and shouting, hardly able to make themselves heard above the crashing of the breakers. Later, exhausted, they had thrown themselves down on the firm sand beneath the shelter of the dunes, gazing at the wide arc of the sky and talked and kissed and talked again.

For a brief while it was as if time stood still, and in all the world there was only the two of them. The shadows that had overhung their visit to Islay had lifted and faded away. It seemed almost impossible that they should ever return.

Chapter Nineteen

Next day all traces of rain had gone, and a cold sun gilded the roofs of the cottages and the smooth surface of the sea. They had booked places on board the Stirling to London train for that evening and Jeff had gone down to the police station to tell Sergeant Brady of their intended departure and to find out if there was any further news. Sally knew that it was only out of consideration for her that he wasn't combing the island like a madman, searching every cottage and croft for Tony Carpenter and his brother and friend, and continuing the search for the elusive Pete Mackay.

There was one thing she wanted to do before she left Islay, and it was something she wanted to do alone, so his absence was, for once, welcome.

With the experience she had already gained of Islay's changeable weather she slipped her raincoat over her arm before walking downstairs and out to the car. Mr Rees was busy loading picnic baskets and canvas chairs into the boot of his car and paused, rubbing his back as she approached.

'Everything all right?' he enquired mildly.

She smiled. 'Yes thank you, Mr Rees. We're going home tonight.'

'And have you accomplished all you wanted to do?'

'No, but I don't think it matters any more. The more I tried to find out, the more difficult ... and unpleasant ... things became, so I'm giving it up. It seems the easiest thing to do,' she finished lamely.

Mr Rees eyed her speculatively. 'Well, only you can know if it's so. Strange how some things can rankle though, for years sometimes, if we don't tidy up all the loose ends when we have the chance.'

'Please don't make me change my mind. It was a difficult enough decision to make.'

He slammed the boot of his car shut and said with a return of his usual joviality, 'And where are you going now? Sightseeing?'

'No ... I don't know if I'm doing the right thing or the wrong thing, but ...'

Mr Rees gazed down at her kindly. 'Dear, dear, what a mess you do get yourself in. Just tell me what it is you're thinking of doing, and I'll tell you whether it's right or wrong.'

'I want to visit Saligo Bay before I leave.'

'That's where your friend was drowned, isn't it?' Mr Rees asked gently.

She nodded and he took out his pipe, packing the tobacco slowly and firmly into the bowl, then he said slowly, 'I imagine that's one of those things that you have to do or it could become a loose end, rankling—at least it could for someone as sensitive as you. Visit it, Miss Craig, then you can leave Islay, putting all that happened in the past where it belongs. In the past.'

She smiled. 'You're very understanding.'

He flushed, coughing to cover his embarrassment. 'Nonsense, child, nonsense. You hurry off and do what you feel you have to do, and then take my advice: put it in the past and forget it.'

He stood at the hotel door, waving to her as she reversed out and turned towards Bruichladdich. She turned inland at Kintraw, enjoying the silence of the moors and her own company. This was what she should have done days ago, and the knowledge gave her peace of mind. The road skirted Loch Gorm, dipping down on the far side of the peninsula to the rough road that she had walked along to Kilchoman church. This time she turned right, catching brief glimpses of the sea as she crossed the rolling green headland to Saligo.

There was nothing there but a large notice in scarlet letters, warning swimmers that bathing was unsafe. The rich green of the hills merged, dipping to the banks of a freshwater stream that ran smoothly down, glittering over its pebbly bed to the sea, still hidden by a bluff.

She slammed the car door behind her and set off towards it. A stiff breeze was blowing and she belted her coat around her, following the banks of the stream towards the roar of the ocean. It didn't take her long. The stream widened, spilling out over silver sand, losing itself among the foaming shallows of the bay. It was a horseshoe shape, the rocks and boulders that formed the arms curving round steeply, the whole force of the mighty Atlantic pounding against them, the spray raining down on her as the water sucked and swirled, racing up towards her feet, covering the sand with a sparkling sheen.

She sat down on one of the damp rocks, eyes closed, head leant on the cliff behind her. The roaring of the waves filled her ears and the tears fell fast and freely down her cheeks, in a silent farewell to Miranda. When at last she rose and turned her back on the white-crested mountains of water curling and plunging, she felt drained, purged. Unseeingly she made her way back to the car and it wasn't until she had reached the turn-off for Kilchoman again that she gave any thought as to where she was heading.

She glanced at her watch. It was still only eleven o'clock, and she didn't want anyone's company, not even Jeff's, for a little while longer.

This time she drove up the bumpy and unmade track towards the church, leaving the car parked at the signpost for the naval cemetery. With her mind still on Miranda and memories of the past, she strolled unthinkingly out across the grassy meadow that led to the white walled enclosure.

Grazing cows gazed benevolently at her, wandering idly away as she passed by them. Ahead, the silhouette of a white granite cross rose magnificently against the backdrop of sky at the very edge of the cliffs. A small stone wall protected the immaculately kept grass and the neat two and a half lines of identical headstones. She caught herself thinking what a nice cemetery it was and smiled. She'd said that not so long ago to Miranda when they had been on holiday in Brittany and she had managed to drag her round a small medieval church in an isolated country village. Miranda had raised her eyes to heaven, said there was no such thing as a *nice* cemetery, and why did she have to get lumbered with an acute case of melancholia for a friend, and for goodness sake couldn't they hurry up and get back to Deauville, she had a date at the casino for eight o'clock, and if they didn't hurry she'd never make it.

The low gate squeaked as she pushed it open, but there was no other sound, apart from the distant roar of the sea crashing on the shore hundreds of feet below.

She wandered slowly down the lines of graves, each one carefully tended and planted with flowers. There was G Harris, Petty Officer 3/435676 H.M.S Otranto 6th Oct 1918 age 25 with the inscription *Abide With Me* in small gold letters below, and further on, a grave without a name with the simple inscription A Sailor of the Great War Royal Navy H.M.S Otranto 6th October 1918. Known Unto God. The only grave that varied was that of the captain who had a cross at his head. She crossed over to the granite monument that soared skywards and sat down heavily at its foot. She felt tired, both physically and emotionally: it had been an arduous week and she would be glad to see the end of it.

A bee droned over the scarlet dahlias and purple thyme on the graves and she stretched her feet out in front of her, watching it as it hovered and circled, resting lightly on one flower and then another. In the distance she could see the roof of her car beside the two lonely crofts and the austere building of the church. Immediately behind them soared the gloomy backdrop of the overhanging hills, but away to the left the green fields rolled out, fading away into the rust of moorland and the haze over the distant loch.

A bull stood in solitary splendour in a meadow adjoining the crofts, knee-deep in the drooping silver heads of the wild bog cotton. The bee skimmed her head, then returned to the rich feast of flowers some yards away. She watched it idly as it settled on an anemone, the cloud of scent drifting across to her.

The grave was like all the others, small and neat with its uniform headstone. Pete Mackay Petty Officer 2/3434 H.M.S Otranto 6th Oct 1918 age 19. Never Forgotten.

She pressed the back of one shaking hand to her mouth, her heart beating so hard that she thought her chest would burst. Her legs were too weak for her to walk over to have a closer look, but there was no need. The letters showed quite clearly. Here was the Pete Mackay that Miranda had meant her to find, the one place on the island that she would be sure she would come to. The picture of the soiled gardening gloves in Miranda's drawer sprang to mind, the gloves that were so out of keeping with the rest of Miranda's belongings . . . gloves that had been used for digging . . .

'Oh, my God,' she whispered, biting her hand till it hurt. Forcing herself, she looked at the soil at the foot of the headstone, at the begonias and marigolds that the bee was still hovering above. The earth was a shade darker than on the other graves, as if it had been freshly dug, as if someone had recently patted it all down again, someone in a hurry, for dried crumbs of soil sprinkled the smooth grass on either side.

Her mind raced wildly as she tried to think, to understand, but it was no use. Her brain seemed paralysed, crippled by fear. Unsteadily, she rose to her feet, giving the grave a wide berth as she walked with faltering footsteps to the wrought-iron gate. She had to tell Jeff. She had to find him quickly, now, this very minute. Jeff would know what to do. Something like hysteria rose in her throat, threatening to break loose as she began to run, flying over the rough grass as if the devil himself were at her heels.

Chapter Twenty

It seemed to take her an eternity to open the car door, to put the key in the ignition. An endless age to reverse and bucket down the narrow track to the road, and all the time her mind was crowded with unbidden images of Miranda digging up the grave of a seaman dead for over fifty years, of herself having to take the same pair of gloves, having to desecrate the grave herself . . .

'No, no, *no!*' she said savagely, feeling her panic mounting, knowing that at any minute her self-control would break. 'There has to be a reason, a simple, logical, acceptable *reason.*'

She swung the car round on to the road, pressing her foot down hard on the accelerator. Jeff would know. Jeff would handle it . . .

She closed her mind to everything but the road in front of her, praying that she wouldn't meet another car as she forced the engine to the limit, whipping round the sudden bends, down the straight stretch that skirted the loch, sweeping past an isolated croft. Ahead of her, tucked away at the roadside, was the scarlet flash of a telephone box . . .

She braked hard, gouging up clouds of dust behind her, the tyres screaming to a halt. She was trembling so much that she couldn't open her shoulder-bag. Fumbling like a two-year-old she struggled with the fastener, emptying the contents on the seat beside her, then, grabbing her purse with sweaty fingers, she ran across to the kiosk.

The number of the hotel . . . she gazed at the instructions on the wall facing her, her mind a complete blank. What was the number? Surely she could remember it . . . With a sob she turned to the directory, flicking through the pages . . . if she couldn't find it, she could always ring the operator ... dial the police ... the number was there. With relief she leant against the kiosk wall, dialling with nervous fingers.

The familiar voice of the receptionist answered, and Sally said, in a voice that sounded to herself surprisingly calm, 'Could I speak to Mr Roberts, please?'

'Just one moment.' The girl on the other end of the line sounded happy and carefree, a whole world away from her.

'Would you hold, please? Mr Roberts won't be a moment.'

'Tell him it's Miss Craig and that it's urgent,' Sally said, struggling to sound normal and sane.

Jeff's voice said, 'Hallo, is that you, Sal?'

'Oh Jeff, thank goodness. Jeff I've found him, Pete Mackay ...'

'You've *what?*'

The door behind was wrenched open, and before she could even turn, a gloved hand covered her mouth, jerking her head back, while something hard and metallic dug into the middle of her back.

'Tell him,' a familiar voice said, 'that you're out sight-seeing and won't be back for dinner, but that he's not to worry.' Her head was wrenched back another painful two degrees. 'And if you don't, then I'll have no alternative but to shoot you.'

Jeff's voice was saying, 'Sally, what's the matter, are you there? Sally ...'

She said hopelessly, 'I'm here Jeff, I ... won't be back till after dinner.'

'What do you mean, you won't be back? Why? What's this about Pete Mackay?'

'I'll explain when I see you, Jeff. 'Bye.'

The phone was taken from her hand and put back on the rest. She turned and Tony Carpenter said pleasantly, 'So you've found Pete Mackay. I am glad. It will save us all a lot of unnecessary trouble.'

He tossed the gun lightly from one hand to another and then put it away in his pocket.

'Come along, let's go somewhere to talk that's a little more congenial, but I'll need your keys.'

A motor-bike lay tossed in the hedgerow, the wheels still spinning.

Helplessly she handed over her keys and sat in the passenger seat. He smiled at her, the blue eyes light and cold.

'And who is Pete Mackay?'

She closed her mouth firmly, staring straight ahead as the car picked up speed.

'Don't be annoying, darling. Remember the movies. We have ways of making you talk, you know.'

'And Miranda?'

'Miranda,' he said, 'was a very silly girl.'

She folded her arms across her stomach, concentrating on where he was taking her, memorizing the route. They swept down to the main road that skirted the head of Loch Indaal, then turned up a side road towards the moors and the distant hills.

Tony seemed to find the silence no hardship, and turned on the radio, humming to the music as they travelled further and further inland. With a sinking heart Sally searched the landscape for houses or crofts, for telegraph wires, anything that would indicate the presence of other people. There was nothing, only the vast expanse of peat and heather and bare outcrops of rock as the ground grew hillier and stonier.

He smiled. 'The only person you have to blame for all this is Miranda. She brought it all on herself ... and you.'

Sally stared mutely out of the window. High up above the hills, a huge bird, looking suspiciously like an eagle, swooped down on its prey. Sally watched uncaringly, the hopelessness of her situation becoming increasingly clear as they climbed higher and higher.

'I'm afraid your car isn't built for ground like this, which is why I left mine so conveniently handy.'

The Range Rover was parked at the entrance to a gully that ran up between steep hills. Obediently and without speaking she slammed the car door and climbed into the Rover.

He said lightly, 'It's not a bit of use sulking and being childish. All we want to know is where Miranda hid the stuff, and only your Pete Mackay knows that.'

'Stuff?' Sally said. 'What stuff?'

'Sorry. I keep forgetting. You're still in blissful ignorance, aren't you? Not to worry. Another few minutes and I'll explain everything to you.'

'Like you did before?' she asked bitterly.

He laughed. 'I was rather good, wasn't I? You even believed all that about Miranda and Gregory being lovers. But I couldn't have you reporting us to the police. Here we are. Home sweet home.'

Ahead was a tumbledown croft, sheltering under an overhang of rock.

'Not very comfortable I'm afraid, but there again, it's your fault entirely. If you hadn't followed me to the farm we'd still be there.'

The door opened and the man who had knocked her unconscious in An Cala stood at the doorway.

'Has she talked?' he shouted across.

'Not yet, but she will.'

The horror and panic she had felt on seeing the grave had disappeared. Now she only felt numb, like someone walking in a dream: everything that was happening to her was unreal, a hideous mistake . . .

The croft was scarcely habitable and crammed with broken chairs and a filthy table, three sleeping bags lay on a freshly swept section of the floor and beside them was a primus stove.

'Where's Scott?' Tony asked, sitting carefully down on one of the sleeping bags.

'Out the back. Where's the stuff?'

'*That*, Dave, you are just about to find out.'

Another man, the one who had followed her back to Port Charlotte, came in, rubbing his hands and slamming the door shut behind him. He stopped suddenly on seeing Sally, his eyebrows raised.

Tony waved a careless hand. 'Scott, Sally. Sally, Scott. Now that introductions are complete, let's get down to business.' His voice changed, the flippancy disappearing. 'Who, and where, is Pete Mackay?'

The other two men remained standing but it was the slim Tony, carefully avoiding contact with any of the dust and dirt in the croft, who commanded the situation. Anger licked through Sally, suppressing any fear and making her defiant. She stood in the centre of the room, and stared coldly from one man to another, letting the contempt she felt show. The man named Dave eased his weight from one foot to another, averting his eyes from her gaze to look at his watch. Scott Carpenter gave Sally a cursory glance, and in the dark blue eyes there was something that looked very much like sympathy. He was larger and more heavily built than Tony, and with his sun-tanned skin and fair hair looked the sort of man that Miranda might have been attracted to, temporarily.

Tony's voice cut into her thoughts. 'Put the stuff in the car, Dave, we're going.'

'She hasn't said anything yet,' Dave pointed out reasonably.

Tony laughed. 'She doesn't need to. I know. Now put the gear in the car and let's get out of this God-forsaken hole.'

Dave opened his mouth to speak again, thought better of it, and began picking up the sleeping bags and primus stove.

'What happened?' Scott asked quietly, his eyes still on Sally.

Tony laughed, springing agilely to his feet and dusting his trousers down with his hand as Dave disappeared outside.

'She went to the Bay and then up to the naval cemetery. I parked near the crofts and watched through the binoculars.'

'And . . .'

'She wandered down the graves and then sat at the foot of the monument and as she did so . . .' Tony's voice lost its gaiety. 'As she did so she suddenly sprang to her feet like that'—he snapped his fingers close to her face—'and began to run for the road and her car, and when I say run I mean run.'

He gazed speculatively at her. 'I must admit I was foxed for a few minutes, but then, following her as she drove at about a hundred and sixty, it all clicked into place. She'd found Pete Mackay all right, and the stuff. It's buried in the cemetery. Isn't it, Miss Craig?'

Sally didn't reply but continued to stare at him contemptuously, head held high.

Tony began to laugh again. 'And the damned thing is, she still doesn't know what's it about!'

There was another silence. She looked across at Scott Carpenter, who seemed to be growing more uncomfortable with every passing minute.

Tony went on. 'However, in the few minutes we have left, it will give me great pleasure to enlighten you. The car that Miranda drove back from Turkey had forty pounds of heroin stowed away in it. It was quite simple. All I had to do was collect the car and its contents when Miranda reached London, but unfortunately Miranda was too quick for us. When I collected the car and stripped it, there was nothing there.' He shrugged. 'It was obvious to a child of three that she'd cottoned on to what was happening and removed the stuff herself . . .' He broke off and looked out of the window to where Dave was busily stowing things into the back of the Range Rover. 'She didn't go to the police though. She had three million dollars of dope in her possession and the temptation was too much. She brought it here, to hide until she could dispose of it, and we followed . . .'

Sally spoke for the first time. 'You're wrong. She wasn't trying to sell it herself . . .'

'For God's sake, grow up,' Tony said exasperatedly. 'Anyway, what her intentions were don't matter. She had it and we wanted it, and now, thanks to you, we have it.'

She could feel Scott's eyes on her and without turning to meet them she knew that the sympathy she had first seen had been real enough. Tony Carpenter had no intention of allowing her to tell anyone of what had happened. Finding Pete Mackay's grave had signed her death warrant.

Dave put his head round the door. 'We're ready.'

'What,' Sally asked, struggling to keep her voice steady, 'are you going to do with me?'

'I'm afraid we shall have to make sure you stay here until we have had ample time to leave the island . . . and Great Britain. The rope, Dave,' he said, without taking his eyes from her face.

'And I'm supposed to just stand here and let you tie me up and leave me to starve, miles from anywhere?'

He moved across to her, a coil of heavy twine in his hands.

'Be sensible, Sally, there's no alternative. Twenty-four hours is all we need. I'll see to it that someone is told when we're safe out of the country.'

'No!' she backed away, her heart hammering painfully, her mouth dry.

'It's the only way. We'll leave you a sleeping bag, you'll be all right.'

She was against the wall now, her hands flat against the crumbling plaster. The panic that she had held at bay was beginning to rise now, washing over her in swamping waves, threatening to engulf her completely. She strove to remain calm, to keep hold of her senses. She said in a voice she hardly recognized, 'It would take me days to walk back to Bridgend. You could be miles away then, there's no need for the rope ...'

'Sorry, darling,' Tony said, grasping her wrist and swinging her away from the wall, doubling her arm behind her back. She twisted violently as he pulled her against him, struggling and fighting with feet and teeth. He swore as she kicked his shin bone hard, twisting free for a brief second before he wrenched her back, knocking her against the wall, twisting her arms painfully higher ... Within minutes she was bound hand and foot and lying on the dirty floor. Tony stood panting and rubbing his shin. He swore again as he straightened up, slicking his hair back with his hand and tucking his shirt back into his trousers.

She wanted to scream, to hurl abuse, but her breath was squeezed out of her body and then it was too late. The door slammed after them and they were gone.

Seconds later the Range Rover's engine surged into life and roared off down the steep hillside. The only sound left was that of her own laboured breathing and the north wind whistling down the chimney.

Chapter Twenty-One

Her cheek was pressed against the cold damp stone of the floor, her hands and ankles lashed securely. On the floor a few yards away was a sleeping bag that Dave had tossed through the door before they left. The constriction in her throat and chest was so tight that she could hardly breathe. From outside came the silence of miles and miles of deserted countryside, with not a hope of help.

A strangled sob escaped her and for a brief second she teetered on the brink of complete hysteria. Then, struggling to compose herself, to grab at the last vestiges of calm, she forced herself to breathe more deeply, to think, think . . .

Tony Carpenter had no idea that she and Jeff had gone to the police, that much had been obvious. They would collect the heroin, make for the ferry . . . and be arrested. Then they'd have to tell where she was. They'd *have* to. A large black spider scuttled across the far corner of the room, then hung on to the ledge of the broken skirting board, gazing, it seemed to Sally, malevolently at her. It seemed to know that she was helpless; any minute and it would be across to her, creeping round her, spinning a web.

She shut her eyes, biting her lip so hard that she cut the flesh, then her senses were sharpened to another danger, a danger that made her forget all about the spider.

On the still, dry air that hung in the croft, there came the faint whiff of smoke. She twisted her head, sniffing the air. The smell was unmistakable. She scanned the floor for a dropped cigarette end and, as she did so, a faint wisp of smoke blew gently into the room through the adjoining inner door.

It curled languidly in a thin blue wreath, then, as it began to drift away into nothingness, a fresh puff, this time stronger and more pungent, curled its way high into the air. Mesmerized, she lay still, watching as it swirled and eddied. Then there was another sound: the brittle crackle of fire.

This time there was no holding back the terror. It drowned her completely as she rubbed her wrists frantically against the sharp, cutting edge of the rope, straining with every fibre of her being to set herself free. She was praying now, chafing one bloodied wrist against another as the smell and sound of fire grew stronger. Smoke was pouring into the room in a steady stream, making her cough and her eyes sting, and all the time the dreadful sound of flames licking hungrily at wood grew louder and louder.

The heat became palpable and a sudden flurry of sparks shot through the open door, flicking and then dying on the stone slabs. The rope wasn't giving an inch. Pain seared her wrists as she twisted and twisted, the twine cutting deeper and deeper into her bleeding flesh. The bare walls were lit by a rosy glow, then tongues of flame licked round the door, eating the dry wood in giant leaps, the smoke choking her, blinding her so that she couldn't see. The heat scorched her legs and she forced herself over, rolling away, but the wall was only a yard away and there was nowhere else to roll to. A noise like the sudden rushing of wind swept the roof and showers of sparks fell to the floor, smouldering on the sleeping bag, missing her by inches.

'Dear God, please, *please*,' she prayed incoherently, the heat unbearable, the vivid leaps of red and gold shooting along the skirting boards, the plaster falling as the beams caught hold. Then she felt the rope give, not much, just a bare slackening. She held her breath, tugging with all her strength, then she stopped pulling against the twine; this time she slid her upper hand agonizingly round till it lay immediately above the other, then, her thumb pressed into her palm, her fingers cramped together, she eased it upwards. The rope pressed unyieldingly into her thumb bone, then slowly, scraping her skin off as it did so, she pulled it higher. Centimetre by centimetre she drew her hand out of the biting rope. Blood was seeping slowly over the backs of both her hands and she knew that she would never be able to undo the knots that bound her feet.

The heat in the room was almost unbearable, the smoke choking and blinding. Unsteadily she tried to rise to her feet and hop to the door but her ankles had been tied too securely for her to stand. Heavily she fell to the floor, her hair catching the flames that engulfed the lower part of the walls, frantically she shook her head, beating at it with her hands, then she saw her handbag a few feet away from her.

Hardly able to breathe, to see, she groped for its blistered surface, pulling it towards her. Her numbed fingers closed round her make-up bag, tugged at the zip, scattering the contents, her nail scissors fell bright and shining to the scorched flags.

Semi-consciously she sawed at the rope around her ankles, then she faced what had been the door. Swaying, she covered her head and body with the smouldering sleeping bag and ran blindly towards and through it, throwing herself over and over on the springy turf, free at last from the heat and flames and the choking, suffocating smoke.

She rolled free of the burning sleeping bag, lying face downwards on the cool, blessedly cool, grass. There was a sudden rushing of air and as she turned her head towards the croft the roof caved in, gold flames leaping high as it burned furiously.

With a sob she buried her face once more in the sweet-smelling grass, huge shudders shaking her body until at last she lay spent and exhausted.

After a little while she pulled herself weakly to a sitting position, gently fingering her cut wrists where the blood had congealed. Painfully she tore at the seam of her underslip, making make-shift bandages, then, unsteadily, she rose to her feet and began to walk away from the still burning croft towards the distant valley. Gradually as her strength returned she began to walk quicker, hurrying towards the point where Tony Carpenter had made her leave her car for the Range Rover.

The track that the Range Rover had made was still quite clear and she followed it blindly, oblivious to her surroundings, until she reached her car, dearly familiar and dependable and in working order, the keys where she had left them in the ignition, the door still open.

Wearily she eased herself behind the wheel, nursing her throbbing wrists, one thought only in her mind: to reach the safety of Jeff's arms and never, ever to leave.

The drive to Port Charlotte could only have taken twenty minutes, but it seemed to Sally to take a lifetime. The blood was slowly seeping through her bandages and every movement of her hands on the wheel brought a fresh wince of pain. The thought of his nearness filled her with fresh strength and she ran at once to the hotel, inside asking breathlessly for Jeff at the reception desk. As the receptionist stared at her with horrified eyes she realized for the first time what a mess she must look, her hair singed, her face smoke-blackened, her wrists bound in rags of blood-stained lingerie.

She said again, urgently, 'Is Mr Roberts in, please?'

The girl continued to stare stupidly and Sally turned, heading towards his room. As she did so, Mr Rees came running across the lounge towards her.

'Good God, girl! Whatever's happened to you?'

'Oh, Mr Rees, is Jeff in the hotel?'

He gripped her shoulders, steadying her. 'What's the matter? Have you crashed?'

'I must see Jeff . . . is he here?' She tried to break free but he held her firm.

'Just a minute, you're not fit to go anywhere.'

'But I must.' She wrenched herself free and he said, 'He was in a state, looking for you. I told him you'd set off to go to Saligo Bay—and he's not back yet.'

She groaned and he put his arm around her shoulder again. 'Look here, my dear, you need a strong drink . . .'

She shook her head. 'I'm sorry, Mr Rees. I have to go. I'll explain later.'

'Miss Craig . . .' he called after her, his brows knitted in a worried frown, but the hotel door slammed shut behind her, leaving the receptionist and a handful of other guests gazing after her in stunned amazement.

She didn't have the strength to go chasing after Jeff to Saligo Bay, and besides she never wanted to see that part of the island again. Instead, she went straight to the police station, telling her story as briefly and concisely as possible to an unbelieving constable.

'You'd better come with me to see Sergeant Brady,' he said at last. 'He's over at the farm. Then we'd better get you to a doctor, or would you rather see the doctor first?'

She shook her head. 'There are men watching the airport and ferry, aren't they? I mean, there's no chance of them getting away?'

The constable was only about twenty and completely flustered by having a girl on his hands with a story of three million dollars' worth of heroin and being burned alive. He said vaguely, 'If that's what the Sergeant said he'd do, then I expect that's what he's done. I don't rightly know. I've been away for three days' leave and . . .'

'Let's see the Sergeant,' Sally said with growing anxiety. 'Quickly.'

Chapter Twenty-Two

'Sergeant knows all about it, does he then?' the young constable asked wonderingly.

'He doesn't know about the heroin,' Sally answered shortly, wondering if any check at all was being kept to prevent Tony Carpenter and his friends from leaving Islay. She sat hunched in her coat, willing him to drive faster: after the speed she had been used to travelling in the last couple of days, his brisk forty-miles-an-hour seemed like a snail's pace.

'But he'll be knowin' who you are?' he asked carefully.

'Of course he'll know who I am,' Sally snapped. 'I'm not some sort of nutcase. What I told you was the truth. They did try to burn me to death and they *do* have three million dollars of heroin on them.'

'From a grave?' he asked ingenuously.

'From a grave,' Sally said firmly. 'Look, can't we go a bit faster?'

'Ach, this is as fast as you can go on these lanes.'

She didn't bother to contradict him.

He swung off the main road, cutting across towards Loch Gruinart, while tension built up inside her. If the constable hadn't been briefed about the search for the men, then the chances were that the island's police weren't taking the breaking-in of An Cala and her previous suspicions very seriously.

She almost shouted aloud when the gaunt stone outline of the farm and its broken-down outbuildings came into view, and she found herself crossing her fingers as the constable slowed down to allow three cows to lumber lazily out of the road, and then swung round, parking outside the high privet hedge that fenced off the unkept garden.

She didn't wait for him to get out of the car, but pushed open her door and ran towards the house.

The Sergeant, seeing the car draw up, was on the doorstep to meet her.

'Miss Craig, what on earth . . .'

'Are there men checking the airport and ferry?' she gasped, dreading the reply.

'Ach, lassie, of course. There's no need for you to be worryin', but what's happened to your hands?. . .'

'It's heroin,' she said, feeling weak with sudden relief. 'Miranda had hidden it in one of the graves in the naval cemetery—Pete Mackay's grave.'

'Heroin!' the Sergeant said, his eyes riveted on hers.

'Miranda was in Turkey for a couple of months. When she came back, Tony Carpenter and his brother had used her to smuggle forty pounds of the stuff out of the country in a Range Rover. Only she found it and removed it herself and brought it here with her. Gregory Phillips was in on it. He came here after her, and then, after their deaths, Carpenter and his friends came searching for their lost property.' She took a deep breath. 'They've just left me tied in an isolated croft miles from anywhere, and to make sure I didn't tell anyone, very thoughtfully set fire to it.'

The Sergeant's face shuttered. Taking her arm, he said, 'The rest will do later, Miss Craig. You need a doctor. Harris!' The young constable jumped to attention. 'I'm going straight back to the station. You take Miss Craig away over to Doctor Burnett and then bring her back to me, and be quick about it.'

Sergeant Brady sprinted out to his car, with Sally and the constable following a little way behind. As the Sergeant reversed sharply down on to the road, a movement at the far side of the loch caught her eye. A dark green dot was speeding rapidly seawards. The constable opened the door for her and she said suddenly, 'Have you any binoculars?'

With the air of a man who refused to be surprised by anything she might request, he said, 'In the glove compartment, miss.'

It was impossible. It couldn't be them, not in a hundred years ... She raised the glasses to her eyes, focusing unsteadily. She couldn't see the occupants but the car was a Range Rover.

'Oh, my God, it's them, it's *them!*' She clutched at his arm and he pressed his hand on the siren of the car, bringing the speeding Sergeant to a skidding halt and a rough turn round, the cows running away in dismay as the engine revved and he careered back. Slamming his door, he ran tight-lipped towards them.

'The lady says it's them, sir, over the other side of the loch.'

'What the devil ...' He snatched the glasses from her hand. Following the moving dot as it sped out towards the point, then he pushed them back into her hand. 'You absolutely sure?'

'They had a Range Rover ... it has to be them.'

'Get Campbell and Larkins, and get them out on to Ardnave Point, I'm going round there now. You watch them from this side.'

He sprinted back to his car and the constable called his colleagues on the intercom. Then, face flushed with excitement, he proceeded to contradict what he had said about forty-miles-an-hour being his top speed as he raced after them towards the sea.

Despite the bucketings of the car, Sally kept the glasses pressed to her eyes, never leaving the green car as it flashed along the water's edge and out to the cliffs.

'Further on, miss, can you see?'

She moved the glasses, scanning the road ahead of the parallel car. The small figure on the thin line of shingle was indistinguishable, but the sleek lines of the speed-boat bobbing a few yards away from his feet, and the motor-bike slung down on the top of the bank above him, were not.

'They're going to get away! After all this, they're going to get away!'

'Don't you worry, miss,' the constable said grimly. 'They'll not get far. We'll have them picked up before they reach dry land again.'

The gap between car and boat was narrowing. As she flicked

the glasses back, she caught sight of another car bearing down at high speed behind.

'Sergeant Brady, he's right behind!'

The constable took his eyes briefly from the road. 'That's not him, it isn't a police car.'

She rested her arm on the back of the seat, trying to keep the glasses as steady as possible, the wind from the open window blowing her hair wildly across her face. Impatiently she pushed it back, focusing on the car that was gaining so rapidly on Tony Carpenter.

She might have known. She should have known. Should have expected it, but the shock hit her like a sledge hammer, driving all her breath and strength from her.

'Oh no, *no!*' she whispered, eyes riveted with horror as Jeff's car bore down on its prey.

'What's that?' the constable asked, weaving at high speed over the pitted track.

'It's Jeff. He's following them, and I know they have a gun . . .'

The constable swung the car round on to a spit of land opposite where the boat was moored. He took the glasses from her, and then handed them back, calling headquarters on the intercom. Sally didn't hear what he said. She was oblivious to everything but the drama being enacted on the far side of the shimmering water.

She felt the point at which Jeff must have first seen the boat, realized their intentions. He went flat out, zooming after them like a maniac. Then there was the crack of a gun and the sound of shattering glass carried clearly across the loch as Jeff's windscreen disintegrated, and the other car slowed down as it approached the boat. The car veered sickeningly then righted, still pressing on. Sally's head roared and her heart was thumping so loudly that it threatened to choke her, then with a sob of terror she saw Jeff only yards from the other car, hunched over the wheel, screaming down on to it.

His car smashed into the rear of the Range Rover, the sound filling the stillness of the afternoon, then the Range Rover plunged off the bank, somersaulting over and crashing roof-downwards on to the sand and shingle. Jeff's car sped on, embedding itself nose first into the undergrowth, back wheels lifted clear, spinning wildly, then there was the roar of an explosion and flames shot yards into the air, engulfing Jeff's car in a vortex of fire.

She screamed as she struggled to get out of the car. Then she was running down to the water's edge, the world crashing about her, the nightmare come true. Dimly she was aware of the constable's voice, of his restraining arms, before her legs buckled and she fell down into a merciful abyss.

Chapter Twenty-Three

The lounge of the hotel had been commandeered by the police. There was Mr Rees, puffing attentively on his pipe, Sergeant Brady, looking grim yet pleased with himself, Constable Harris oozing importance; three other policemen that Sally had not previously met, herself, freshly bandaged and washed, and Jeff, ugly stitches across his forehead, one arm in a sling, but looking as cool and calm as if the only thing in question was a minor traffic offence.

Dave was kicking his heels in the island's tiny gaol, Scott Carpenter was in hospital with a fractured skull and multiple injuries, and Tony Carpenter was dead.

Sergeant Brady was polite and patient but wanted the whole story again, from the minute Miranda left Turkey to the point where Jeff smashed into Tony Carpenter's car and then scrambled clear of his own before it burst into flames. It took a long time and several cups of coffee and all the time, marring the exquisite relief and happiness Sally felt at Jeff's presence, was the dark possibility that he would be charged with Tony's manslaughter.

The Sergeant listened attentively to him as he explained for the third time what had happened when she had telephoned him at the point of Tony Carpenter's gun.

'We'd arranged to leave the island on the evening ferry. You will remember we told you that ourselves when we saw you earlier in the day.' The Sergeant nodded and Jeff continued. 'It was obvious that something was wrong with Sally over the phone. She told me she'd found Pete Mackay, then her voice altered, was strained, tense. She said she wouldn't be back for dinner and rang off. Well, for a start, we weren't *having* dinner on the island, we hoped to be half-way to the mainland by that time ... I drove to all the places I could think of, the shop where she had stopped before, Bridgend, but there was no sign of her. When I got back here I saw Mr Rees and he told me she'd been going to Saligo Bay when she'd set off.

'I drove straight there but she wasn't there, then I continued up the road towards Kilchoman. As I did so, I saw Carpenter and another fellow speed down the road from the church and the naval cemetery and turn right. I just *knew* something had happened to Sally and that they were behind it, so I followed. I kept my distance at first, then, when they began to skirt Loch Gruinart, I drew closer. I was determined not to lose them. I wanted to talk to them, to find out what had happened to Sally.' He paused, looking across at her. 'Then I saw the boat. My only intention was to catch up with them before they reached it, but one of them, the guy in the passenger seat, turned and fired at me. Now people don't do that without good reason, and at that moment I truly believed they'd killed Sally. Why, I hadn't the faintest idea, but I don't believe I thought straight after that. My only aim was to stop them.'

'Which you did admirably,' Sergeant Brady said dryly. 'I think, in the circumstances, and with Constable Harris as witness to the shots fired at you, you will hear no more on that score. No charges at any rate. The heroin was packed in polythene bags and in a leather holdall on the back seat of the car. At the moment it's resting amongst our lost property but someone is flying from the mainland to take it off our hands. As to Miss Taylor's part in this affair ...'

'I think I can help you there,' Sally interrupted quietly. 'She'd gone to Turkey and had a casual affair with Scott Carpenter. When she discovered the heroin in the car, I don't think she believed Scott Carpenter would do that to her, or that Tony was involved. The sentence for smuggling drugs from Turkey is death, and whoever planted them in the car she was driving knew that was the sentence she would receive if caught. I think she took the stuff out of the car, intending to hand it over to Tony for him to try and find out who *had* planted it. After all, it was obvious they'd soon be looking for it. As soon as she knew who it was she would have reported it, but unfortunately she didn't get the chance.'

The Sergeant nodded. 'That, in the circumstances, would probably be the best view to take of the affair ... and I think that an early night is in order for you, Miss Craig.' He rose stiffly to his feet. 'I'm afraid you'll have to go all over this again in the morning when the mainland people get here, but we'll leave you for now. Good night, Miss Craig, Mr Roberts ...'

Sally leant back, comfortable and relaxed against Jeff's protective arm, while Mr Rees poured another coffee for her. The lounge, bereft of all policemen, was suddenly empty and very quiet.

'All this happening, and all I've been doing is potter about megalithic tombstones!' he said, handing her her cup.

'A very sensible and sane occupation,' Sally said drowsily, her cheek pressed into Jeff's shoulder.

'And what,' Jeff said teasingly, 'do you know about anything that's sensible and sane? To go haring off by yourself ...'

'I know, I know,' she said. 'Of all the silly, stupid ...'

'Lovable ...' He kissed her temple and Mr Rees coughed uncomfortably.

'I think I'd better be toddling off now, see you in the morning, before you leave.'

'Has Pearl White invited you to the wedding?' Jeff asked.

'Wedding?' Mr Rees said, beaming with pleasure.

'Wedding?' Sally echoed.

'Didn't I tell you?' he said, hazel eyes meeting hers. 'I arranged for the banns to be called whilst I was in London. We are to be married on the 20th. Unless, of course, you have any objections?'

'No,' said Sally, cheeks flushed. 'I have no objections. None at all.'